PR 6003 .A7 R3

Barker, Dudley
Ransom for a nude

MAY 1991

APR '77

FEB '82

KVCC KALAMAZOO VALLEY COMMUNITY COLLEGE LIBRARY

24721

Ransom for a Nude

by the same author

OUTBREAK

FLOOD

Ransom for a Nude

Lionel Black

STEIN AND DAY/*Publishers*/New York

First published in the United States of America by
Stein and Day/*Publishers* 1972
Copyright © Lionel Black, 1972
Library of Congress Catalog Card No. 72-81209
All rights reserved
Printed in the United States of America
Stein and Day/*Publishers*/7 East 48 Street, New York, N.Y. 10017
ISBN 0-8128-1491-6

y
Ransom for a Nude

CHAPTER I

It was the girl who thought of it first.

'I believe we could get away with it,' she said quietly, contemplatively.

'Get away with what?' the man asked.

'The picture.'

The man smiled. Then, realizing that perhaps she was not joking, slowly annulled the smile, staring at her. Sprawled comfortably, but still elegantly on the scarlet plush of the Victorian chaise-longue, amid the bric-à-brac, the junk and the stacks of old paintings that littered even the man's living-room, she gazed lazily back at him. She was never dramatic or emotional. Sensual, yes—that he well knew—but without emotion. You could say, he reflected, that the sensuality showed in the darkness of hair, the paleness of skin, the slightly thickened lips that she had painted out with a flesh colour. Her name was Euphrosyne Teague, and he often thought that by her looks she might have been Greek. But she was not; her father had been a Greek scholar, held the chair of classical studies in one of the outlying universities. Everybody called her Frosso.

'You mean, steal it?' the man asked. 'But, my sweet idiot, even supposing we could, what could we then possibly do with it? Just now it must be the most publicized painting in the world.'

'Oh yes, of course,' she nodded. 'Charles has seen to that, since it was he who discovered it. He couldn't be more ecstatic if he'd actually painted it.'

She would know, since she was Charles Harrison's secretary—one of the group of wonderfully pretty, off-handedly arrogant, debutante-style girls who decorated the fine, old-fashioned premises of Crosby's, those sale rooms lying between St James's and Bond Street—among the best-known fine-art auction rooms in the world. So she had from Harrison first-hand the story that afterwards spread across every newspaper in the western world—how Harrison, one of the younger men of the firm, had been sent to Sawdon Hall in Dorset when that eccentric baronet, Sir David Bullen, had called them in to see whether there was anything worth selling among the family possessions; and how, even under the thick varnish and the grime, he had appreciated at once the treasure in the old gilt frame, carelessly stored in a loft that, thank God, was not damp. Even the expert they summoned had hesitated before he dared to mutter, with a shake in his voice, 'Velazquez? Could it possibly be?'

It was put, of course, to every test—radio-carbon, X-rays, the chronology of the pigments, analysis of the radio isotopes and the rest. The chemists at the Frobisher Institute of Fine Arts—where they had laboratories equipped to determine the age of pigments and canvas as efficient as those of the National Gallery—admitted, at the end of it all, that at any rate the date was right, it was not a forgery. But Velazquez? Could it be?

When it had been reverently cleaned, there were those who asked, instead, how it could possibly not be. There she lay, on the silken couch cover; the same girl as the Venus of the National Gallery's *Venus and Cupid*. But the mirror was pushed aside, the drapery behind was blue, and the girl herself had turned towards the artist, so that the serenity of the face was directly painted, and one breast exquisitely exposed. It was Harrison himself who had triumphantly hit on the title that was now current throughout the world, the *Venus Revealed*. There were carping experts who canvassed the view that it was a Mazo; but they were a minority. On the best, the most scholarly, most trustworthy authority, this was the work, not of the son-in-law, but of Don Diego Rodriguez de Silva y Velasquez, the master himself.

So how much was it worth? Two million pounds must be an underestimate, Charles Harrison reckoned. He told Frosso so several times; he could think of little else.

The man staring at Frosso in the living-room above his antique shop (much of it junk) and small art gallery (as he liked to call it) just off the King's Road in Chelsea, knew very well the value placed on the painting. His name, by the way, was Sebastian Hurley. He had once been a small-part actor, nothing much. Then an aunt, widow of a rural dean, died in Scarborough and left him enough to start this junkshop-picture gallery, which kept him. In the Chelsea manner he had named the place 'Pleasures'. The name was written in sprawled golden Gothic on the grimy shop window. The shop did little direct trade; the whole area is spattered with such shops. But in the antiques business there are —how can one put it?—side interests which, with discretion, can be remarkably profitable; largely a question of not asking too rigorously where this piece or that came from, and not keeping too accurate a record of where it then went to—especially silver.

Of course he knew the value of the painting; everybody knew. When the *Venus Revealed* went up at Crosby's, and the senior partner, with a rose in his lapel, began the bidding, it must run up to well over two million.

But that was its value in a legitimate sale. If it were stolen, would it have any value at all? Sebastian Hurley would have no moral objections to stealing it. He had few moral objections to anything, except discomfort. But even if he could sustain sufficient nerve to make such a theft, what on earth would be the use?

'How could anyone possibly buy it?' he asked her, beginning to think once more that it was a joke. 'All those famous American millionaires who are mad art-lovers, and buy stolen masterpieces to store in deep cellars beneath the sands of Texas, don't actually exist, darling, you know.'

She looked at him for a moment without saying anything. Lying there on the chaise-longue she had, he whimsically thought, something of the look of the Venus herself. At her age, there was as yet no outer sign of coarseness.

Then she said, slowly, 'Of course we couldn't sell it to anybody. But we could hold it to ransom.'

Now he stared at her, dazed. As the idea sank in, a shudder of terror, of sheer funk, went through him. And yet . . . and yet, was it possible? For somebody who had the nerve, was it perhaps possible?

It was the girl who thought of it first. 'They'd have to pay, wouldn't they?' she said.

CHAPTER II

The three men wandering round Crosby's sale rooms with Charles Harrison might have been a deputation from some small provincial museum looking for a few minor purchases with the ratepayers' money; or representatives of a building firm getting out an estimate for sadly-needed redecoration. Nobody paid any attention to them as they moved slowly through the huge, shabby rooms hung with paintings (many of them surprisingly poor, dirty old canvases), and furnished with straight-backed chairs lined up in rows to face the little pulpits where the auctioneers stood on sale days. It wasn't a sale day. Nondescript groups of people were strolling through the rooms, some with catalogues open, staring at the paintings. Porters in green baize aprons staggered in now and again, bearing some huge gilt-framed study of highland scenery, or of a dramatic moment in the history of sixteenth-century Venice. In one room a group of obvious experts were examining a collection of coins in glass-topped cases, watched with a casual air by one of the uniformed attendants. Throughout the scene languidly fluttered the girl secretaries, bundles of flimsy papers grasped in their manicured fingers, to the smiling approval of the youngest of the three visitors; very pretty girls indeed, he noted to himself, but perhaps a bit above his class.

Passing through the office complex on the floor above the sale rooms, Charles Harrison led them up a narrow flight of stone stairs to the attic level. Opening the centre door of three along the corridor, he showed the men into a bare room with no windows, but only a skylight in the ceiling. 'This is where the picture will be on the night before the sale. It's a sort of tradition.' He smiled gently. 'At any rate, it's useful publicity. The newspapers always carry the photograph of the picture propped up on that kitchen chair, the bare room, and the auctioneer sitting on this other kitchen chair, keeping an all-night vigil. This time, it'll be me.'

'Will you be armed, sir?' asked one of the older men, Chief Detective-Superintendent Francis Foy from Scotland Yard.

'Good heavens, no. We simply rely on Mr Finch here—' he gestured towards the older man—'to ensure that nobody can get anywhere near.'

'Happy about that, Graham?' asked Foy. He and Graham Finch were old friends, former colleagues at the Yard until Finch retired and took on the job of chief operations officer to one of the commercial security firms. Foy had come along, on crime-prevention duty, to offer any advice he could.

'It's not the ideal place,' Finch admitted, 'but I think we've got it covered. I'll set up a control room in the office immediately below, in touch with one man in every other office by intercom. The door at the head of this staircase is steel-clad and will be bolted and barred. Two men here in the corridor. The rooms on either side are simply store rooms, crammed with stuff. We'll station one man in each room.

'The weak spot is the roof. It's a pitched roof, but quite easy to scramble over. There are three main access ways leading to this skylight. Let's go up and look.'

A fire-exit door at the end of the corridor opened on to a small iron platform, with a short iron staircase leading upwards to the roof, across which fire-escape catwalks rambled. Foy gazed round at the untidy London rooftop scene. The only practical access was from the neighbouring roof to the left; to the right was a thirty-foot drop.

'We're co-operating with the building on the left,' said Finch. 'The lower floors are a jeweller's, and damn secure. We've got permission to station men on the two office floors above. If anybody did succeed in getting up on to this roof, there are these three catwalks which could be used to reach the skylight of the picture room. I'll have a man on each, in touch with me at control.'

Foy looked interrogatively at the youngest policeman. 'Any comments, Sergeant?'

'It's not ideal, sir,' replied Detective-Sergeant Ronald Madge. 'A really determined bunch could get through to the skylight.'

'But then what?' demanded Finch. 'To get away, they've got to go down, either through this building or the next. There's no alternative. Unless,' he added with a grin, 'they use a helicopter.'

'Possible.'

'Oh come,' protested Finch, 'we've got to be reasonable. I suppose they could bring tanks down Bond Street and flush us out with napalm. But after all, Francis, it's only a picture said to be worth a couple of million quid. It isn't the Crown jewels.'

Foy nodded. 'Fair enough.'

In Harrison's office, Foy said, 'I think you've got, for all likely contingencies, a reasonably safe room. The picture'll be safe once it's here. But it has to get here, and it has to be taken away.'

'It's Mr Finch's job to get it here,' replied Harrison. 'As you know, it's now on short loan to the National Gallery, and drawing the crowds. It's quite safe there, of course. There are pictures much more valuable than that in the National Gallery, year in, year out.'

'We've got a decoy vehicle, and an armoured van that looks like an ordinary butcher's delivery van, to get it from Trafalgar Square to here,' said Finch. 'I don't think there's any real problem, Francis, particularly if you lay on police motor-cycle escorts to the decoy.'

'It's arranged. And on the night itself, Mr Harrison, I'll see that there are police cars on instant call.'

'Thank you, gentlemen,' said Harrison. He had pressed the buzzer beneath his desk. To the girl who came in he said, 'Bring the sherry, Frosso.'

She came back with decanter and glasses on a small silver tray and handed round the sherry as Harrison poured it.

'Then there's the other end,' Foy reminded him, 'taking the picture away.'

'Doesn't worry us,' replied Harrison cheerfully. 'Once the hammer falls, it belongs to the purchaser—who will certainly be one of the big New York dealers, probably Wildenstein, or perhaps Hymans. They have insurance arrangements, usually with Lloyds, that cover directly the purchase is made. Lloyds have an excellent security officer, who takes over.'

'Then why don't Lloyds come into security arrangements for getting it here, and while it's here?'

Harrison smiled amiably. 'I'll tell you a secret. It isn't insured. Thank you, Frosso. Leave the decanter. I tried to persuade the owner to cover it, but he wouldn't. Gave us a formal letter that the responsibility is his.'

'Premiums too steep?'

'Steep, of course. But I don't think that was the reason. It belongs, as you know, to a baronet with a place in Dorset. Sir David Bullen. And he's a very odd bird. I got the impression he was trusting in Providence. I assure you, a very odd bird indeed.'

An odd bird, Harrison pondered, as his train sauntered through the Dorset countryside towards Dorchester.

Since he had been a bomber commander in the Second World War—one of the three or four most famous of all RAF bomber commanders—Bullen must by now be into his fifties. But with his spare figure, thick brown hair, haughty profile, you might put him at, say, forty; except, perhaps, for the perpetual sadness in his eyes, the air of almost apology.

That was the key to the man. The story went that he had gone to Germany soon after the war, then to Hiroshima, as though compelling himself to a penance, discovering how little damage the bombing had done to military targets and how awful a devastation it had wreaked on towns and townsfolk. Then he had returned to England, resigned his commission, sent back his medals, and thrown open Sawdon Hall to anybody who was homeless.

He had been robbed and abused and swindled, of course, and a couple of times actually assaulted. But he had gone silently on, refusing to be deflected. Gradually one or two people had helped him to regularize the project. The Sawdon Trust had been formed, which could raise charitable money; the Bullen family money had gone into the thing long before. The most notorious of the criminal parasites had been shaken off. Recently the Trust had extended into London, buying a large old house as a hostel in Battersea, renaming it Sawdon House. The thing must be consuming money as a drunkard swallows beer. That, no doubt, was why Bullen had asked Crosby's to see if there were anything in the family relics worth selling—and he, Harrison, had turned up the *Venus Revealed*.

Now the worthy baronet would be able to wallow in good works. As Harrison had no doubt that he would. The Bullens had often, over the centuries, thrown up an eccentric, just as they had even more frequently thrown up a superb fighting man. Harrison knew a bit about them. One of his hobbies was the history of ancient but obscure English county families; it fitted neatly into his profession of selling family heirlooms. There had been a Bullen alongside Wellington in the Peninsula campaign and a mid-Victorian Bullen who had turned Sawdon Hall into headquarters of an odd religious society of flagellants, a scientific Bullen who set up a genetics laboratory in the grounds and succeeded in mating a peacock with a goose (but the progeny would not breed), and a Bullen who had collected a couple of DSOs, and ought to have had a posthumous Victoria Cross when he was killed on the Somme.

In the present baronet, Sir David, the two strands seemed to be entwined.

Waiting for Harrison on Dorchester station was a woman of about thirty, fine features, good brown hair dragged back into a bun, figure plumping a little in a blue suit. She introduced herself as Rose Pearson. 'David sent me to pick you up. He's been shut in with the Trust accountants all day, or he'd have come himself.' She led him towards an elderly Austin parked at the station entrance. 'I'm the sort of head housemaid at Sawdon,' she told him as they started off. 'And when I'm not looking after the guests, as David insists on calling the inmates, I do what I can to look after him.'

Evidently she was in love with him, and probably he hadn't the least notion of it. He was married, Harrison recalled, but the marriage had gone sour soon after the war. Harrison could not recall that there had ever been a divorce, or what had happened to Lady Bullen.

They drove across heathland, then through thickly-wooded lanes. The cottages of the village itself, Sawdon Abbas, were up to the eaves in early roses, clematis and hollyhocks. The pub, the Sawdon Arms, must have been built as soon as the original Hall. That had been burned down in the 1850s, and the replacement, a Victorian Gothic pile, had even yet scarcely weathered into its surroundings. But it was ideal as refuge for the homeless —huge rooms cut up into small units, a communal dining hall, accommodation for scores of families, which were now scattered across the grass of the park, the regiment of shrieking children rushing from one side to the other, and being hauled now and then by vociferous, weary mothers from the lake.

The staff and living quarters were in the one remaining wing of the old Queen Anne house that had not been burned down. 'We all pig in together,' Rose Pearson told him, 'except Lady Mary Bullen, who has a small private flat opening on to the rose garden where none of the guests is allowed.'

'His wife?' asked Harrison, surprised.

'No, no. Sarah, his wife, went back to America.' There was scorn in the woman's voice that confirmed

Harrison's first diagnosis. 'Lady Mary Bullen, his mother. She's elderly now and doesn't really understand the world as it is today. She never fully recovered from her husband's death. He was killed on the Somme only a week after David was born.'

Bullen came out from an inner room to greet Harrison. 'I'm locked up with accountants. We're planning how to spend the money you're going to get us. See you at dinner. Look round and try to find another priceless treasure.'

Harrison smiled. On his previous visits he had made quite sure there were none. Which was as well, he thought, sitting by the window of the bedroom to which he had been shown, looking out over the park towards the lake. A more frightening collection of criminal types than the bunch of 'guests' sprawled on the grass he had never imagined. If there had been anything obvious to steal, it would have gone long ago.

At dinner—Rose Pearson, Charles Harrison, Bullen and a couple of accountants named Henderson and Jocelyn—Bullen talked on and on about the expansion planned with money from the sale. The bank had already advanced him the deposit on a huge, abandoned mansion near Birmingham. Another was mooted in Manchester; and later, if the money were sufficient, yet another near Glasgow. (The dinner itself was execrable. Bullen always took the same food as the guests, from the communal kitchen. The women cooked it by roster. Tonight, Charles thought, must have been a particularly unlucky turn.)

Henderson chaffed him about the extravagances into which he had precipitated Sir David by discovering the painting. 'You'll bust the Trust, Harrison. He'll use all the money to buy more hostels, and there won't be enough to run them.'

'Will the profits be all that huge?' asked Charles. 'How about death duties? How about capital gains tax?'

'I think we're all right on both counts,' said Jocelyn. 'The Inland Revenue would be hard put to it to show that the picture was worth less in April 1965, the starting date for gains tax, than it is today.'

'Granted. But death duties? The painting will have been exempt, I suppose, because it wasn't sold. But now, don't you face duty on the death of every baronet for generations?'

Jocelyn grinned. 'That's the beauty of it. It wasn't exempt. We can prove, on the last three occasions at any rate, that it was valued with the chattels—valued at £50 each time—and death duty was paid each time. Nobody ever suspected it was of any real value, let alone a Velazquez.'

'Why didn't they?' asked Henderson. 'Surely it must have been known when it came into the family.'

'I doubt it,' said Bullen. 'One of the great-great-great-grandfathers—give or take a great or two—picked it up for £20 when he was making the Grand Tour in about 1790. Charles tells me that, at that time, not a lot was known about Velazquez. His paintings were scattered all over Spain, not much thought of, and English travellers collected them for small sums.'

'It's why there are more of them in England than anywhere else outside Spain,' confirmed Charles. 'Or were, until American millionaire tax-avoiders got wise to them.'

'It still seems incredible,' persisted Henderson, 'that nobody spotted the painting for what it is in all the years it was here at Sawdon.'

'That was great-great-grandmamma,' explained Bullen. 'It may have been art, but she thought it disgusting. So up to the attic it went, face to the wall. Nobody ever thought about it again, until Charles Harrison turned it round from the wall and shouted with excitement. Oh yes you did—I heard you. What you actually shouted was Great Beelzebub! Speaks well for your religious training.'

Charles laughed with the rest. 'In my job, Satanism's a great comfort.'

Henderson asked, 'Do you think it will really make more than two million pounds?'

'I'd be surprised if it doesn't. After all, the Velazquez portrait of Pareja which Christie's sold in November 1970 fetched £2,310,000—and that picture isn't a patch on our *Venus Revealed*. On the other hand, the Christie's sale in June of 1971 lowered everybody's sights a bit. Titian's *Actaeon* fell far short of what was anticipated, and Rembrandt's portrait of his son, which is superb, was withdrawn at £160,000. You can never be sure. All the same, I'd be disappointed with less than two-and-a-quarter million.'

'From which,' said Jocelyn, 'you deduct your firm's exorbitant commission of ten per cent.'

'Exorbitant nothing. If you saw our bill for publicity —and that's what really sends the prices up. Believe you me, our PR chaps do a fantastic job in New York—and an even better one, without making too much noise about it, in and around Dallas. Then this time, because David won't let Lloyds in on it, we've agreed to pay for extra security.'

'You're wasting your money,' Bullen told him. 'Who would steal something that couldn't be sold?'

Charles shrugged. 'That's the comforting reassurance, of course. But you never know.'

CHAPTER III

The girl had slid out of bed and was putting on her clothes. She had switched on the electric percolator, so that the smell of coffee was beginning to fill the small room. Sebastian Hurley, groping for the half-empty cigarette packet among the jewel boxes, beetle brooches, china figures in more or less good repair and a jumble of old coins on the table beside the bed, lit a cigarette and leaned back against the pillows, feeling contented. He hadn't to go off to work. His work began when he chose to go downstairs and open the shop; and it didn't much matter what time he did that, or indeed if he did it at all.

Frosso poured the coffee and brought him a cup.

'Thanks. By the way, we've got a man coming to dinner.'

'So?'

'I'll shop for the food and drink. Can you get off a bit early to cook it?'

'Is it so special?'

'Could be,' mused Sebastian. 'He could be the man you want to see.'

'I?'

'You said we'd need help. And when I asked what sort of help, you said tough help. You said I personally wasn't quite the type for anything more violent than a romp between sheets—and you were absolutely right, my dear.'

'Who is he?'

'His name's Hugh Dell—or, anyway, that's the name I was given.'

'How come?'

'I have a few contacts, darling, on, shall we say, the rougher side of the art business. I made a few enquiries . . .'

'You didn't give anything away?' she sharply demanded.

Sebastian stubbed out his cigarette crossly. 'Look here, Frosso, I'm not an absolute idiot. I'm not a bit sure that I'm going through with this thing. But until I decide not to, you've got to trust what I do, and credit me with normal common sense.'

'Sorry,' she said. 'All right, you made some discreet enquiries about finding a man who was tough and not too particular. And the name you got was Hugh Dell. Has he the slightest idea what he's wanted for?'

'None,' he assured her. 'All he knows is that there's a man interested to meet him, to have a talk that might lead to something profitable.'

Frosso looked at her watch. 'I'll have to go in a minute. Tell me all you know about him.'

'It's not much. He has no criminal record, but I'm given the idea that that's because he has never been caught. I'm told he's not known to the police in this country—with the obvious suggestion that he may be elsewhere. They asked, rather pointedly, whether anything would be likely to involve Interpol.'

'And you?'

'I declared with a gay laugh that nothing was contemplated that would, I hoped, involve any sort of police anywhere. They didn't, of course, believe me.

'He's English. He has fought as a mercenary in Africa. He has been waiting around, I am assured, for what is delightfully described as "the big tickle". He'll expect a substantial cut.'

Frosso moved uneasily. 'He sounds too intelligent. Wouldn't it be better simply to hire a thug to do that part of it?'

Sebastian slowly shook his head. 'It's got to be somebody we can rely on not to be stupid. And he has to be as involved as we are, otherwise it could be much too dangerous.'

She turned to leave. 'Well, let's have a look at him tonight. Get something quick to cook. I'll be back as soon as I can. And listen, Sebastian, even if he seems the man we want, there mustn't be the slightest hint tonight what it's about.'

'Run along,' he told her, 'and try not to be silly.'

He was oddly unlike what Frosso had expected.

When she had got back that evening, she had found the shop shut and the room above empty. Sebastian would be over at the pub and had probably taken the man with him. Frosso shrugged and poured herself a vermouth; she was not much of a drinker. She found the steak Sebastian had left soaking in corn oil on a dish and fixed it on the grill, ready. She peered into the fridge to make sure he had vegetables; set out the table for three; then lit a cigarette and settled on a couch under the window from which, looking sideways, she could watch the parade along the King's Road.

She had never before committed a crime; sins in plenty, she wryly told herself (if you could define sin without standards she did not possess), but not a crime. The idea was oddly exciting. She wondered whether all criminals experienced this mental quivering. Was it one of the motives? The only motive really ought to be gain, but she felt curiously indifferent to that. She had not even thought seriously of what she would do when she had the money, or what she wanted it for—nothing in particular. It was just that the idea had come to her, one morning when she was sitting opposite Charles Harrison taking dictation, and had suddenly realized that there was a coincidence that could be used. The realization had jolted her like the jab of a needle. She had the feeling that the whole thing would be a magnificent trip, but active, not passive. She supposed she ought to consider the consequences if it went wrong. But whatever the chances, she refused to heed them. She had tried most things for sensation, but never anything that stimulated her quite so excitingly as this.

She saw Sebastian emerge from the saloon bar with a man, and turned away to get the frozen vegetables out of the fridge. She had everything ready for cooking by the time she heard them coming upstairs.

'This is Hugh Dell,' said Sebastian, 'and this is Frosso.'

'Good evening,' he said.

She had expected some sort of bruiser. But this man might have been a civil servant, or an accountant in the City, or a tutor at her father's old university. He was of only middle height, with a lean body, delicate-looking hands with cared-for fingernails, a long sensitive face with sharply prominent nose and chin, pale grey eyes, blond hair trimmed neatly, like a soldier's. Yes, that was the better likeness; he could have stepped straight out of one of the military clubs. He was dressed, too, with the neatness of, say, a major in an infantry regiment. He was about the age for that, older than she had expected; he must be well into his forties. His voice matched his appearance; that built-in, cultivated tone is acquired only at one of the lesser public schools.

Sebastian was passing round drinks. Dell took whisky. Frosso gestured for another vermouth. Sebastian got himself his usual gin-and-mixed.

'You two go on talking in here,' she said, 'while I cook the dinner.'

Nothing was said of the purpose of the visit until they had finished eating. At table, Sebastian tried to lead Dell into talking of his life as a mercenary. 'He fought with Schramme's men in Rwanda, and for the Nigerians against the Biafrans and with the French chaps in Angola. It's absolutely fascinating—the man of action. Always appeals to a man of inaction, like me.'

But Dell only laughed and turned the talk to antiques and the art business, which soon had Sebastian chatting amusingly. At one moment Frosso suspected that Dell was fishing; he spoke of huge prices paid at art sales, and the sale just coming up of the *Venus Revealed*. But nobody could have told him that she worked at Crosby's. It was natural for the *Venus* to crop up in any conversation about the art business just then.

When they had pushed aside the dishes and were seated in the darkening room, Sebastian got up to offer brandy—but Dell took whisky again and Frosso shook her head—and to switch on a lamp on the floor in one corner.

'As you know,' he said to Dell, settling again, 'it was Freddie who gave me an introduction to you. I expect he told you we are looking for somebody who's prepared to take a few risks, for a substantial fee.'

'I did get a vague hint. What sort of risks? And what fee?'

'One is a bit of kidnapping, as you might put it. For that you'll need a reliable assistant, who need know nothing about the job itself. He'll need to be able to drive a car and it would be useful if he were adept at stealing one. You can pay him whatever the going rate is for that kind of thing, and he won't know anything about either of us—and I expect you would prefer to arrange it so that he doesn't have much direct contact with you either.'

Dell nodded gravely but did not speak.

'The other risk is coping with a security guard. He won't be expecting trouble, he won't be armed, and you'll have me to help you in that part of it.'

'And the fee?'

'Twenty thousand pounds.'

Frosso caught the sudden flicker in Dell's steady gaze, and knew at once that Sebastian had made a bad mistake. The fee was too high. She had an almost overpowering instinct to withdraw from this man, find another. He was too intelligent—and now too alert.

'When is it to be paid,' Dell was asking quietly, 'and how?'

'After the thing succeeds, and in used £5 and £1 notes. It's all right. We're not holding up a bank or anything silly like that.'

'How much in advance?'

'Nothing. And if the thing doesn't succeed, again nothing. There isn't any money unless it does succeed.'

'That,' said Dell with a slight smile, 'sounds like the greatest risk of all.'

Sebastian nodded. 'Probably is. You don't have to be interested, of course.'

There was a long silence. Then, from Dell: 'Suppose I'm sufficiently interested to go one step farther before deciding.'

Sebastian shook his head. 'Not on, old fellow. You either take it, in which case we'll meet again nearer the time to give you the whole scheme. Or you leave it, in which case we'll have had a pleasant dinner party.'

Frosso found herself hoping like hell that the man would say no.

But he didn't.

Getting up to go, he said, 'Let's meet in a few days' time, then—I take it we're fairly close to the date already. Just phone Freddie. I'll be waiting.'

When Sebastian came back upstairs from seeing the man out and locking up, Frosso poured herself a brandy and lit another cigarette, trying not to show her agitation.

'I don't like it,' she told him. 'He's too efficient. It was a mistake to offer him so much. He's already getting ready to double-cross us, I'm sure he is.'

'How can he, darling? He won't have the picture. And he'll be too involved to shop us.'

'We ought to drop him and find somebody else.'

'Look, Frosso,' he said, 'if your nerve's going, we ought to drop the whole thing. We're not in any way committed. All we have is the tape-recording and a few photographs, which can be easily put back. I'm ready to quit now, if you want it that way. My nerves never were particularly steady, sweetheart. But let's be sensible and face facts. The prize is enormous and I believe the scheme is good enough to get it. If we do go ahead, then we have to have criminal help. And Dell's the man. You'll have to accept that from me. I've made all enquiries that are possible, within the limits of discretion. Your objections to him are probably sound. But that's the risk we have to take. They would apply equally to anybody else we got who was efficient enough to do what we want done. Now, do we stop or do we go ahead?'

'I don't know,' she murmured unhappily.

Sebastian went across to kiss her, taking the brandy glass from her, unzipping her dress. 'It's been a difficult day, darling. Come to bed.'

She submitted, although she did not particularly want to. Not that night. She was too involved, somehow, in a different sort of sensation.

But afterwards she was sleepy. She asked him sleepily, 'Sebastian, have you ever committed a crime before?'

Groping for another cigarette amidst the bedside bric-à-brac, he replied, 'That depends, angel, on what exactly you mean by a crime.'

CHAPTER IV

As the staff at Crosby's packed up to go home on the evening before the sale, Graham Finch, chief operations officer of Keepsafe Limited, went round the building posting his men. He wanted the setting as watertight as he could make it before he set off to collect the painting from the National Gallery. He was due there at 19.30 hours. He ought to have the picture inside Crosby's by 20.00. At 20.05 Mr Harrison was due to arrive for night duty. First there was to be the facility for the Press photographers who would be waiting in the salon downstairs. That was timed for 20.30. By 21.00 hours Mr Harrison would be locked in the top-floor room with the painting, to start his night-long vigil, and Finch's men would be stationed on every possible access route, with Finch himself at the control centre on the floor below the top.

Having satisfied himself that every one of his men was in position, and that all the sale-room staff had left the Crosby building, he nodded to his chief aide, a young fellow named Wilkinson, and they went down together to the taxi waiting in the street.

They entered the National Gallery by the works door. Five Keepsafe men were waiting, dressed as porters.

Watching from a window, and timing carefully by his wristwatch, Finch signalled to the first two to start as the Keepsafe security van drew up outside. They hurried out with an empty frame, of correct size, swathed in cloth. Hastily they pushed it into the van, jumped in, slammed the door and the van jerked off, with two police on motor-cycles escorting it.

Finch could spot nobody who seemed to be interested.

In precisely ten minutes the phone at his elbow rang. 'Yes?' It was the man he had left in control at Crosby's. The first frame had arrived and was safely in the building; no sign of any trouble.

'Right,' said Finch, hanging up and waiting. He continued to watch carefully through the window, but could see nothing to alarm him.

He looked at his watch. It was now coming up to 19.50 hours. He could see the nose of the armoured van, got up to look like a butcher's delivery, rounding the corner. He signalled to the three remaining men. They hoisted the second swathed frame—this one with the *Venus* in it—and made for the exit, Finch and Wilkinson crowding in behind them. Against all the rules, Finch had a small-calibre pistol slung in a holster below his left armpit; he dared not contemplate what would follow if he had to use it.

The picture was across the gap and into the van. The three men jumped in after it, pulling the door close quietly behind them. Finch and Wilkinson got quickly into the driving cab. The driver at once set off in a direction away from Crosby's.

So far as Finch could see, nothing suspicious had occurred. Nobody was following them.

Travelling down the Strand, the driver turned into Savoy Street, and through on to the Embankment. They made it through Whitehall Place, Whitehall and Great George Street into the park, cut along behind the Horseguards into the Mall, and thus up St James's towards Piccadilly and Crosby's. The men had the picture out, and into the building, almost before the van had stopped.

Finch looked around. Nobody seemed to be displaying any special interest. He grunted with relief and went inside. The picture had been taken straight to its attic destination, uncovered, and placed on the traditional straight-backed chair, under an electric bulb hanging on a naked flex. Finch took a quick look at it and grunted again. Nice bit of nude, no doubt, but so what? Privately, he couldn't see what all the razmataz was about.

At 20.15 hours he saw Charles Harrison getting out of a taxi at the entrance. He went to meet him. 'Good evening, Mr Harrison. Everything's okay. The picture's in place, and we've had no trouble.'

'Good. I'll go up. Give me ten minutes, then send the photographers up. And you needn't worry about them, Mr Finch. We've known all of them personally for years.'

They came in a bunch and took the inevitable picture —the young man in his chair and the painting on the chair behind him, under the naked bulb.

'You staying here all night, Mr Harrison?'

'Yes, the usual thing.'

'Got something to read?'

He grinned and held up a paperback thriller. The photographers laughed and went off.

'Ready for me to lock up now, Mr Harrison?' asked Finch.

'Sure. Settle down for the night.'

'You've got the alarm switch at your right hand if you want us for anything.'

'Sure. But I doubt if you'll be troubled.'

'Hope not,' said Finch, making his way back to the control room, having first watched the doors being locked behind him. 'Everybody in place?' he asked Wilkinson.

'Yes sir, I've just made a complete tour. Everybody in place.'

So that seemed to be that. The picture and its guardian were in a locked room, surrounded on every side, and at top and bottom, by his own men. Finch felt he could relax at last. But he did not. He was the old-style, plodding policeman. Every five minutes throughout the night he made intercom contact with one or other of the men posted on duty, varying the order in which he rang them. Throughout the night, at intervals of five minutes, one or other of them reported that all was well.

The alarm shrilled at precisely 06.45 hours next morning.

As he ran for the control-room door, Finch shouted to Wilkinson, 'Contact all round'; and heard the crackle of the intercom, and Wilkinson's voice, still calm and deliberate: 'Alarm. Report fast—anything unusual . . . Nothing? Okay, report station by station, alarm order.'

The man posted at the head of the attic stairs was startled to see Finch running up but went straight into the drill—shoved back the bolts on the door, thrust in the key and unlocked without waiting for orders.

'Nobody through here, sir,' he reported as Finch dashed by.

The two guards in the upper corridor were even more startled, but reacted as promptly to the agreed pattern. One ran to unlock the store rooms on either side, to check with the men stationed within them. The other swiftly unlocked the room in which the picture was placed, but did not follow Finch into it, stayed on guard at the open door, calling after him, 'Nobody came through the corridor, sir.'

Harrison, seeming dazed, was slumped forward on his chair, barely holding himself on to it, his right hand still gripping the alarm button, shrilling it convulsively. The picture still stood on the other chair, untouched. The room smelled of chloroform.

Finch quickly put an arm round his shoulders, supporting him back on the chair. His hand fell away from the switch and the alarm buzzer was at last silent.

'What happened, sir?'

Shaking his head as though trying to clear his brain, he muttered, 'I don't know. I think I dozed. Suddenly felt something pressed over my mouth and nose—strong smell. Must have passed out. When I came to just now, I was on the floor.'

Finch glanced sharply round. The thriller Harrison had been reading lay on the floor to his left. Near it lay a pad of cotton waste, impregnated with the chloroform which he could yet smell. His gaze went automatically to the skylight. It was shut, as before; not that that meant much.

Several of the men had now followed him into the room. He motioned to one to get the chloroform pad into polythene. Not that it was likely to be helpful. It was a pad of ordinary cotton wool, probably bought from a chain store.

'Report from control, sir. Every man in position. Nothing suspicious seen by anybody.'

'Tell control, every man to stay in position, exactly where he is now. Get the order round fast.'

The man at the door called his report: 'Both men in the adjoining rooms in position, sir. Nothing seen or heard all night.'

Finch nodded, his gaze returning to the skylight. It must have been the roof. So the only possible explanation must be the connivance of at least one, and probably all three of the men stationed there. His mouth was set in a grim line.

'You all right now, Mr Harrison?' he asked.

'Yes, I think so. Feeling a bit foggy—but yes, I'm okay.'

Finch gestured to one of the emergency-squad men. 'Look after him. You two come with me. I won't be long,' he told the first man. 'Going up on the roof.' To the man at the door he said, 'Repeat to control, no man is to move an inch from where he is now, and I want a report from any guard who sees another guard change position, or has seen any movement outside the ordered patrols throughout the night.'

On the iron fire-escape platform Finch checked to reassure himself that it could not be reached from below; the fire-escape staircase led only upwards, a short flight to the catwalks across the roof immediately above, connecting with the roof next door on the far side; a blank wall, without so much as a small window, dropped away for at least twenty feet to the roof of the adjoining building on the near side. It was possible for an intruder to have been hoisted to the platform on a rope by a man already standing on it. Finch felt an acute dismay. For that would involve two more of his men—the two in the corridor—and still involve the three on the roof. Five of them bribed? Finch felt stunned. Out of the five, he would have felt complete confidence in at least four, and would have trusted a couple with his own safety.

He grunted and made his way up the iron stairs. To Russell, the man guarding the first catwalk, he said, 'You say you've seen nothing suspicious all night?'

'Nothing, sir.'

'Did you leave your post at all?'

'Only once, sir. Went down for a pee at 03.25 hours. Reported to control before I went, sir. I was away five and a half minutes. Reported on return. It'll all be in the control log.'

'The room was broken into,' Finch told him abruptly.

Russell's astonishment seemed genuine. 'Broken into? Not from the roof, sir. Not possible. What time?'

'Never mind that. I want from you, as soon as you can, a written statement of your watch throughout the night. I want it before you go down—everything in detail—without any reference to control to check with the log.'

'Very good, sir,' said Russell stiffly. He understood the way suspicion was pointing.

Finch went on to the two others, Ken Rogers, then Robert Kershaw. The result was much the same—stout assurances that nobody had crossed the roof all night and silent resentment on being ordered to produce written statements without reference to control.

On the third catwalk Finch went over to the skylight. Looking down he could see Harrison and a couple of his own men standing in front of the picture. Harrison made as though to touch it, and Finch saw with approval one of the guards checking him; a chance of fingerprints on the frame, of course. But would any of that be necessary? Since the picture had not been taken, would it even be necessary to call in the police, or make any disclosure at all?

Finch stared thoughtfully across the London rooftops, lit by the early morning sun. That was the most puzzling fact of all—that the picture had not been taken. Why? Had they been interrupted? If so, how, by whom?

Whatever the answer, it did not clear his own men from suspicion. Whether the police were brought in or not, Finch savagely promised himself that he'd find out which of them was involved. How could Keepsafe continue to operate otherwise? How could he hope to keep his own job?

There were no signs of forcing the skylight. It was fastened and bolted from below. Grimly he began to veer to the conclusion that the room must have been entered through the door, which inevitably involved the two guards in the corridor, as well as at least Russell on the roof, and probably the two others too.

He straightened up and made his way back along the catwalks and down the iron stairs, saying nothing to anybody. When he re-entered the room, Harrison was again seated in his chair.

'Feeling better now, sir?'

'Yes, I'm all right now.' From the sound of his voice, he was still under strain.

'At any rate, Mr Harrison,' said Finch as cheerfully as he could manage, 'for some reason that beats me, they've left the picture safe.'

The gaze that swivelled towards him was sombre. 'Do you imagine that anybody would go to such lengths and not take what they were after? Talk sense, man.'

'But . . .' Finch gestured towards the picture on the far chair.

'It's a copy.'

Finch stared at Harrison, then at the picture, then at Harrison again. 'A copy?'

'A damn good one, I'll grant you that. Done by an expert forger. But it still doesn't make sense. How could they possibly have imagined that, in these circumstances, the copy would not be detected? How could they have hoped to get away with the sale of the copy?'

'They, sir? Who do you mean by that?'

'The devil knows. Whoever broke in here and put me out.' His face was looking even graver. 'The sale . . .' He glanced at his watch. 'We've less than five hours. All the imps in hell! What to do?'

'Are you sure it's a copy?' asked Finch.

'As sure as I can be by just looking. I'm supposed to be an expert, Mr Finch. I think, if I'd been shown it casually, I might have been deceived. But, of course, it wouldn't pass any of the laboratory tests. It's a copy all right, Mr Finch—a good forgery, but still a forgery. You can confirm it, by your sort of evidence, by looking at the back of the frame. Oh yes, it's the same frame. They've left us the frame! Can you see the slight scratches round the edge, which must have been made as they took the original canvas out and put the forgery in?'

From the back of the frame, Finch nodded. Then he looked up at the skylight. 'Mr Harrison, when the picture was taken from the frame, could it have been rolled or folded?'

'Not without detaching the canvas from the stretcher—and the risk of damage would have been terrible.'

Finch looked up again at the skylight. It seemed more likely than ever that the entrance and exit had been the door.

Then he cursed himself for an oversight and ran to the nearest intercom phone. 'Wilkinson, send all the spare men you can find to this floor. I want both adjoining rooms, and any other nook or cranny, thoroughly searched.'

'What are they looking for?'

'The picture.'

'The picture? But . . .'

'A duplicate. See if there's a duplicate anywhere.'

Harrison was on his feet again and seemed to have shaken off the numbing effect of the anaesthetic.

'Mr Finch, I'm coming to my senses at last. In less than four and a half hours, the *Venus Revealed* was to have been offered for sale at what was likely to have been the auction of the century. The most famous dealers in the world would have come thousands of miles to bid for it, and there are at least half a dozen millionaires, nearly all of them American, who are panting to spend a large fortune on it. And what we have now is a forgery. That is, I know it's a forgery, but we can't cancel the sale on my sole opinion. It has to be verified by scientific tests—and I have less than four and a half hours to get that done. I'm not sure it's even possible. But one thing is certain. I haven't five minutes to waste.'

'I don't think I'm following you, Mr Harrison.'

'I've got to get that picture to the Frobisher Institute lab, and get the experts working on it, within the next half-hour.'

'You can't move it, sir. We've got to call the police straight away. They won't have anything moved.'

'You've all seen what the situation is. What else could the police want?'

'Fingerprints, for one thing.'

'Would the frame do?'

'Yes, I suppose so,' hesitated Finch.

'Right. Get a couple of your men wearing gloves, or whatever, to hold the frame, and I'll take the canvas out from the back. I suppose it won't matter if my prints are on anything.'

'No. We can take yours later, and eliminate those.'

'First of all, will one of your men do some telephoning for me?'

'Jenkins. Give him your instructions, Mr Harrison.'

'Mr Jenkins, you know my office? Good. In the top left-hand drawer, which is unlocked, you'll find my telephone-numbers pad. First telephone my secretary, Miss Teague, and tell her to get here as fast as she can and don't wait for asking questions. Once she's here, she can handle the avalanche that'll break over us all. But before she comes, ring Dr Humphrey Evans at his private number—it's somewhere in Knightsbridge, you'll find the address and phone number on my pad. Tell him Charles Harrison begs him to go round to the Frobisher at once—in his pyjamas if necessary. Tell him, on my authority, that it's the worst crisis he'll ever hear of. Ask him to ring up his best experts and get them to the lab as fast as he can. Got that? And ask him to ring the Institute to warn the caretaker that I'm coming round in a few minutes with a picture, and he's to admit me. If it's the usual night man, he'll know me. But it might be somebody else. Tell Dr Evans that I'll explain all the rest when we meet there. That's all.'

Jenkins hurried off downstairs. Finch, unhappily watching Harrison's expert fingers detaching the canvas from the frame, asked, 'Shall we get one of our armoured vehicles round to take you? It could be here in half an hour or less.'

'We haven't got half an hour to spare. Send one of your men with me. Tell him to nip out and get a taxi. The Institute is only just the other side of Oxford Street. A taxi's the simplest way.' He had detached the canvas now and was fastening round it the cover in which it had been brought to the room. 'And, Mr Finch, directly Frosso gets here—that's my secretary, Miss Teague—tell her what has happened, and to telephone at once to all three of the senior partners and inform them. They'll know what to do about the sale cancellation. If they want me, say to ring Humphrey Evans at the lab.'

One of the guards reported, 'Taxi ready, sir.'

Still unhappily, Finch watched Harrison take the picture, aided by Fenton, the man to accompany him, and make for the stairway to the head of the goods lift. One of the men who had been searching came to report that there was no duplicate of the picture anywhere on that floor. Finch went down to his control room and got through to Scotland Yard. 'Is that you, Francis?'

'No, sir. This is Sergeant Madge. Is that Mr Finch? The Super's on his way in now, sir. I'm expecting him in about a quarter of an hour. Everything all right, sir?'

It was a question Finch did not want to answer even to himself, let alone to anybody else. But there was no help for it. 'Afraid not, Sergeant. The picture's gone.' He heard Madge's soft, astonished whistle. 'I don't know how, and I can't imagine where. I have to bring you in, of course. But I don't suppose fifteen minutes will make much difference. Ask Mr Foy to get in touch directly he arrives.'

'Certainly, sir,' said Madge. 'I'll leave him a note. I'm coming straight round, in case I can be of any use to you. I know the Super would want me to be there as fast as possible.'

'Thanks,' said Finch, putting down the phone. Then he sat at his desk, doodling on the blotter. The question he could no longer avoid was, how had they got the picture away?

It had not gone down through the Crosby building, of that he was certain. So it must have gone out over the roof, or been lowered from the fire-escape platform to the roof of the next building on that side. That was for Foy to investigate. But it meant there was no doubt of the complicity of at least two, and probably five of his men. Finch grunted and felt for his pipe, his pouch, his matches. He could not take it in. He simply could not believe it.

\.

CHAPTER V

The avalanche that Harrison had forecast started with the arrival of Sergeant Madge. He was there within five minutes of putting down the telephone.

Finch asked, 'You've started the routine?'

'Yes, sir. But I've suggested holding up action until Mr Foy gets there. Can I have a look around upstairs?'

Finch gestured to one of his men to take Madge to the attic floor. 'He'll tell you all we know as yet, which isn't much.'

Next came Harrison's secretary, Miss Teague. Finch admired the way she took the news; no gasps or silly questions, just a sudden look of surprise, then she got down to phoning the senior partners. Finch heard her begin, then left her to it. She was capable of handling that side of it herself, that girl. She was already soothing the old man who must be having a sort of apoplexy at the other end of the phone.

'The only thing is,' she was saying into the phone in her languid voice, 'that if we start cancelling publicly now, the Press will have it within minutes . . . Yes, I know, but even if we tell one or two of the biggest dealers, it's absolutely bound to be public in half an hour . . . Oh, if you would come straight in, Mr Syndercombe, I'd be so relieved. Mr Harrison has taken the forgery round to the Institute to have a quick check. He left a message that he couldn't take the responsibility of cancelling the sale on his unsupported opinion that the picture had been switched, he had to have scientific confirmation of it . . . He'll be very glad to know that you approve.'

Finch went back to the control desk and settled to the written reports which had come down from the men on the roof. He ordered similar reports from the two who had been stationed in the upper corridor. He started to make detailed comparisons, checking against the control night log. Now that he had his second wind, he realized that chasing wasn't going to find the picture. The best hope was to pin down discrepancies in the reports of the men, some of whom must have been involved—he repeated that grimly to himself, they must have been. Then he would tackle them separately, striking from strength. It should not be difficult to break one of them down and get a lead that a week of hunting through London would not provide, simply by pointing out discrepancies in their reports that proved them to be lying.

Unfortunately, he could not find any discrepancies.

But it simply was not possible for anybody to have broken through his cordon and got into that room, and out with the picture, without the connivance of at least some of the men in the building. That had to mean

Keepsafe men, since they were the only ones.

At that moment Finch stopped puffing at his pipe, laid it carefully in the ashtray on the desk, and stared at the shininess of the telephone. He had suddenly realized that Keepsafe men were not the only ones. There had been one other—Mr Harrison. Was it possible that Harrison himself was involved? In what way involved, or for what purpose, Finch could not for the present guess. But the hairs of his thick old neck were prickling. There was reason, he thought, to have a different kind of conversation with Mr Harrison.

Finch walked through into Harrison's office and waited for a moment until his girl put down the phone.

'Could you get me the Frobisher Institute, miss?' he asked. 'I want a quick word with Mr Harrison.'

Miss Teague nodded and dialled the number. 'Is that the Frobisher? Who is speaking? Oh, the caretaker. Has Dr Humphrey Evans arrived yet? Could I speak to him, please? It's rather urgent. It's Mr Harrison's secretary at Crosby's . . . Hallo, is that Dr Evans? Miss Teague here. If Mr Harrison isn't actually in the lab yet, could he please have a word with his office? What? Oh, I see. Thank you, I expect we'll call him later.'

Looking at Finch, she told him, 'Mr Harrison hasn't arrived there yet, Mr Finch. It's rather odd. He shouldn't have taken as long as this.'

A messenger from control: 'Chief Superintendent Foy on the line for you.'

Finch hurried back. 'Hallo, Francis. Got your sergeant's note?'

'Yes. I'll be with you in a few minutes. And, Graham, at the Marylebone station they've got a taxi-driver with an odd story that seems to involve your place. I've told them to bring him round to me at Crosby's.'

Behind Foy came the usual crowd of police experts,

photographers, fingerprint men and such. Police cars were gathering at the entrance. Syndercombe, the first of the senior partners to reach the building, came in to protest. 'Will you please shift the bunch of policemen outside? They're attracting so much attention, the newspapers are bound to get on to it soon. We haven't decided yet our policy for the sale. The news simply mustn't get out until we have.'

Foy nodded sympathetically and gestured to Madge. 'Disperse the lot from outside. Give my instructions to the technicians to get through as soon as they can and then leave unobtrusively. We'll do all we can to keep quiet, Mr Syndercombe. But we can't hold the position for long.'

'No more can we,' replied Syndercombe. 'The sale is timed for 11.30. Within a couple of hours or so, every art dealer of importance in the world, and half the world's experts, will be entering this building, expecting to see the great Velazquez *Venus* sold. By then we're going to have to tell them something. But what? Will somebody please tell me exactly what has occurred?'

From Foy: 'Graham, you'd better brief us both. Is there an office, Mr Syndercombe, where Mr Finch can tell you and me about it in complete privacy?'

Syndercombe led them to an annexe to his own office. They settled round a small table, and Finch carefully, doggedly, related all he knew about the night. At the end of his account there was a long silence. Then Syndercombe asked, 'So what do you think has happened to the Velazquez?'

Finch was silent. Foy asked, 'Is there any possibility, Mr Syndercombe, of selling that painting anywhere in the world?'

'Shouldn't have thought so.'

'Nor I. Of course, it could be a madman, with some grudge against society.'

'Damn' smart madman,' cut in Finch.

'Odd things do happen. There was that fellow who got himself locked in the National Gallery some years ago and made off with a painting.'

Finch shook his head. 'This couldn't have been done without inside help.'

'Besides,' pointed out Syndercombe, 'where would a lunatic get a first-rate copy of a Velazquez that has been on view for only a few months? That could be the best lead you have, Superintendent.'

'You mean . . .?'

'According to what Charles Harrison told Mr Finch, it's a good copy, an excellent forgery, so far as the naked eye goes. There are not more than three men in the world who could have painted such a forgery, and we know who they are—and doubtless the international police network knows where they are. Whoever did it must have done it after Charles discovered the original down in Dorset. It went on view at the National Gallery only that short time ago. The forger must have been in London during that time, to study the original. It couldn't have been done from any of the colour reproductions—not done well enough, at any rate, to get an alpha from Charles Harrison.'

'That's probably the best lead we've had yet, Mr Syndercombe.'

'It can be bettered. When Charles returns with the laboratory report on the forgery, we'll know so much about it that we shall probably be able to say who it was that painted it. Each well-known forger has certain little characteristics, you understand. By the way, has Charles come through with anything yet?'

Finch hesitantly replied, 'Last time we enquired at the Institute he hadn't arrived with the picture, although he had plenty of time to get there.'

'Then where the devil is he?'

A knock on the door, and Sergeant Madge: 'Taxi-driver's here, sir.'

The taxi-driver came in; typical stalwart London taxi-driver. 'Name of Hodgson,' he announced himself. 'The coppers at Marylebone've got all my details, and I've given 'em a signed statement.'

'Thank you, Mr Hodgson,' said Foy. 'We'll get that in due course. But it'd help a lot if you'd be good enough to tell us here, quite simply, just what happened.'

The taxi-driver settled to the table. He was enjoying this.

'I was coming down from Bond Street direction this morning when a chap hailed me and brought me along to Crosby's.'

'That was Fenton,' cut in Finch, 'the man I sent with Mr Harrison.'

'He said there was a picture to take round to some place in Manchester Square. Few minutes later he and another chap came out, carrying this picture all wrapped up—never saw the picture myself.'

'The other man,' said Finch, 'was Mr Harrison.'

'They took the picture in the back with them. Blocked my view into the cab, but I was all right for driving, with wing mirrors. The second chap told me to drive towards Manchester Square, and when we got near, he'd direct me. When I got across Oxford Street, I was going straight to Manchester Square, but he told me to turn left and cut through Portman Square to George Street. He said he wanted to get to the back entrance of some Institute, in that little mews off George Street, just behind Manchester Square—a little cul-de-sac place.'

'Was there anything parked in the mews?' asked Foy.

The taxi-driver looked at him with respect. 'That's just it, guv. There was a little green van about half-way in, slewed across a bit, like. I pulled up and called to the driver to draw over, but there didn't seem to be any driver. I was just going to get out to have a look-see, when there was this scuffle in the back of my cab. I couldn't see what was going on—the picture was blocking my view. So I called out, "Here, what's up then?" When a chap suddenly bobbed up beside me in the mews, with a cosh in his fist. "One word, mate, and you'll get it," he says. I couldn't see what he looked like. He'd got a funny mask on, like you have at parties. So I kept quiet and got my head down, like this chap told me to. Naturally, I couldn't see much more. What I did see was that the picture was being lifted out of my cab by one of the fellows that brought it, and shoved in the back of the little green van. Then this fellow got in the van and drove off, hell of a lick, turned left into George Street, and away.

'As he went, the fellow with the mask gave me a sudden shove—knocked me right down on to the luggage shelf. By the time I got up again, and got my wind back, this chap was running out of the mews. He turned right into George Street. I wasn't able to see what he looked like because, although he pulled the mask off his head, he had his back to me. I was going to start up my cab and chase him, but then I saw he'd whipped the ignition key and taken it with him.

'Anyway, then there was this sort of groan from the back. And there on the floor was this fellow, who'd hired me—knocked clean out, with blood coming out of his mouth. Jeez, I thought he was dead.'

'Fenton?' asked Finch anxiously.

'He's been taken to Middlesex hospital, sir,' said Madge. 'He's still out—concussion. But the doctors say they think he'll be all right.'

'He was in a nasty mess,' went on the taxi-driver. 'I run over to the nearest phone booth, to call the police and an ambulance. Bloody thing was smashed up, like so many are. But luckily there was a copper passing the end of the mews and when I yelled he came running. So then the coppers took over, and there's only one thing still bothers me.'

'Which is?'

'I'm still clocked on. There must be a couple of quid on it by now. Who pays my fare?'

'I'll see you get it from the cashier here before you leave,' said Syndercombe.

'Marylebone got through to the Yard, of course, sir,' Madge told Foy. 'They alerted the patrols, but no trace of the green van, no trace of Harrison.'

Syndercombe, elbows on table, chin resting on clasped hands, had an air of bewilderment on his elderly, handsome face. He pushed his fingers through the greying wings of hair brushed back from either temple. He gestured with his hands in dismay. 'Charles? Is it being suggested that Charles has taken the *Venus*? Oh, but that's absurd. Quite aside from the certainty that he would never do such a thing, there's the fact that it would be valueless to him if he did.'

'Or to anybody else, Mr Syndercombe,' put in Foy.

'But Charles Harrison—oh, impossible. He's one of our own people. And anyway, Superintendent, why on earth should Charles steal what he knew to be a forgery?'

'In a rather confused situation, Mr Syndercombe, I think one probability is becoming clearer—that it wasn't a forgery. It was the original.'

'I simply don't understand.'

Foy sighed. 'It's much too early for categorical statements. But it would have been very difficult, unless half of Finch's men were heavily bribed, to have got into that room last night with a forgery and out again with the original picture.

'But it would not have been specially difficult for the man already inside to stage an attack on himself, declare as an expert that the picture which was still standing in position was a copy which must have been switched for the original while he was unconscious—and then, on the pretext of having it scientifically examined, walking out with it under everybody's nose.'

Syndercombe's face had gone a deep shade of grey. 'But why should he have done it? Why?'

Foy shrugged. 'We don't know. But I think there's one simple question that will tell us whether Mr Harrison staged the whole thing and, for some reason as yet unexplained, has got away with the genuine Velazquez. And it's a question to which you, Mr Syndercombe, will probably know the answer. Is there in fact a rear entrance to the Institute in the mews off George Street into which Harrison directed the taxi?'

Syndercombe stared at him. Then, as the implication became clear, slowly and painfully shook his head. 'No, Superintendent,' he admitted, 'there isn't.'

CHAPTER VI

Foy got through to the Yard. The taxi-driver had not noted the registration number of the green van. But it must have been recently stolen and would doubtless soon be identified, and a little later found abandoned somewhere.

There was Harrison's bachelor house in a South Kensington mews to be examined, but a patrol reported that it was locked and empty, and the authority for going over it had not yet been obtained.

Technical reports on the room from which the picture had been taken added some weight to Foy's assumptions. The skylight had not been opened that night, or for many weeks previously. On the frame of the picture were the prints of several hands. Some must have been made by Harrison when he removed the canvas, the rest were probably porters'. Inconclusive, because any unauthorized person who had handled the frame could have been gloved.

In his own office Syndercombe was facing the problems of the sale. Already some of the chairs in the Great Room were filling up. Soon the big dealers would be arriving. It was not possible to alert them all; better, perhaps, to wait until the sale opened and then make the announcement that the Velazquez for which they had all come so far, had gone. Syndercombe, usually a man of decision, found himself unable to make up his mind. The thought overwhelmed him that it must be Charles who... He sat at his desk, doing nothing, staring at his silver calendar and the point of light reflected from the lid of his silver inkwell, as though he were on the point of hypnosis.

It was Charles's secretary who broke him out of it. 'Yes, Frosso, what is it?'

'Don't you think that somebody ought to inform Sir David Bullen?'

Syndercombe actually struck his forehead with his fist, in a theatrical gesture which would normally have horrified him. 'I must be leaving my senses. Do you know where Sir David is?'

'He'll be at the hostel he has opened in Battersea. Sawdon House, he calls it.'

'On the phone?'

'Oh yes, and I have the number. But don't you think it might be better...'

'You're right. But I can't undertake it myself, I simply

haven't the time—or the strength, Frosso, or the strength. Has Mr Grant arrived yet?'

'Just arrived.'

'Please tell him what has occurred and ask him to go to Sawdon House to tell Sir David personally. Nothing less is possible, you're perfectly right. And, Frosso, beg Mr Grant not to come to me for details. I'm at the end of my rope.'

As she went out to brief Geoffrey Grant, the second senior partner, Syndercombe felt a strong desire to question her about Charles. Surely, if he were really the author of this mad exploit, there must have been some signs, some indication, that he was capable of behaving like a lunatic. But he checked himself; after all, Frosso didn't know that Charles was suspected of being the person who had actually . . . Syndercombe shuddered and sank his forehead once more upon his open palm.

By shortly after eleven o'clock the Great Room was packed, humming with excitement. Possibly there had never been such a concentrated gathering of famous dealers, millionaires, art critics and experts, and chosen Society, in the whole history of fine-art auctions.

Weeks before, Syndercombe had laughingly challenged his opposite numbers at both Christie's and Sotheby's to rival it from their records, and they had been hard put to it to find anything comparable.

In agony Syndercombe retreated from the small window through which he could survey the Great Room, and returned to his office. He took a large gulp of neat Scotch and tried to reassemble his calmness, his suavity. When the time came to go out and make the announcement, he would be the man to do so. He would delegate that awful task to nobody. Then in the afternoon he would send in his resignation from the firm and retire to the cottage in Suffolk where he had intended to spend his last years—but not for some time to come. He recalled the auctioneer who, many years before, had catalogued a book at a country-house sale as 'Works of William Shakespeare in one volume,' and sold it for a fiver. And when it turned out to be a First Folio, had committed suicide. However, Syndercombe assured himself he need not go that far. Resignation would suffice.

The gaunt, sepulchral face of Geoffrey Grant peered into the office. 'Well, I've told the owner.'

'How did he take it?'

'With astonishing calm. He had a Miss Pearson with him—his secretary, I think, or the manageress of his hostels. I put the fact bluntly on the table, without preliminaries. I thought that best.

'"Stolen, Mr Grant?" he asked me. "By whom?"

'I told him that nothing was yet known for certain. We didn't know who the thief was—if, indeed, there were a thief—or precisely what had happened.

'Then the woman, Miss Pearson, said, "You'll get it back, David." And Sir David gave a sort of smile—but a grave sort of smile, if you follow me. He looked at Miss Pearson and said quietly, "Oh yes, Rose, we'll get it back. Far too much depends on it. We'll get it back." There didn't seem to be anything more to say.'

'Have a drink,' said Syndercombe, gesturing towards the cabinet in his office.

'Thanks,' said Grant gratefully. He poured himself a stiff scotch.

Syndercombe looked at the sedate old grandfather clock against his office wall. It was time. He carefully arranged in his buttonhole the rose he selected from a vase on his desk. Then he turned and, without a word, went down the stairs and into the Great Room, climbing with his customary dignity on to the rostrum.

The scene that he faced in the Great Room would, in any other circumstances, have given Syndercombe the keenest pleasure of his working life. There is perhaps, as he had once remarked, nothing so exciting in the civilized world as a great sale room tensed for the auction of some superb masterpiece of art. Even the starters lined up for a classic horse-race are less exciting; for that is merely a contest of the muscle and stamina of animals and the physical skills of undersized, unintelligent men.

Whereas in a great sale such as this, the contestants are the shrewdest brains engaged in perhaps the most intricate business of dealing in the world, fortified by the sensitive perceptions of the finest and most highly-trained intellects among art critics and historians, and backed by the wealth of men who, in their single lifetimes, have acquired such massive fortunes that, if taken together, their resources would rival that of a medium-sized nation.

And the prize is no bag of guineas and the hope of stud fees, but the glorious achievement of some one of the most superb of the choicest of all men—the artists. Where is there any contest, short of battle, comparable in emotion and excitement?

All these thoughts sped through Syndercombe's mind as he took his station on the rostrum and faced the room.

Never had he faced quite so distinguished a gathering. The great dealers, of course—all of those he knew. His eye wandered along the front rows. There were the expected men from New York, from Paris, from Hamburg, scattered among the familiar London dealers from the square mile or less that enclosed the Great Room, as it were, as its centre, its living heart. All these men were not only Syndercombe's most valued business associates, with whose affairs he was on intimate terms and whose methods he knew precisely, down to the idiosyncratic bidding codes and practices of each individual; many of them were also his personal friends. All that, he sadly commented to himself, would end that morning.

Looking beyond the dealers he could see a few of the men who were backing them, and envisage those who were present only in the form of blank cheques. They were nearly all oil millionaires; curious how mankind has permitted the discovery of the most essential natural fuel of its planet to enrich almost beyond imagination a few men who would otherwise have been bartenders or racing touts in Texas, or unwashed petty chieftains of unconsidered tribesmen, their tents loaded on their half-famished beasts, wandering from one Arabian waterhole to the next. Contact with them he would not unduly regret losing.

All these were only the front fringe of the assembly in the Great Room. To one side, where the snouts of the television cameras were probing, were mostly grouped the newspapermen. Gathered in little rival groups were the art scholars and historians, many of them from the great galleries and museums of two continents. And the bulk of the rest of the crowd consisted of the curious who were rich enough, or well enough connected, to get a place in the Great Room for such a momentous sale. One or two of the leading politicians, Syndercombe briefly saw; some magnificently beautiful women who must be Americans, or actresses, or both; several notable peers and a duchess; three or four eminent men of letters; and half a dozen of the leading painters and sculptors of the decade.

The chatter in the room had abated a little as Syndercombe entered, but then risen to a crescendo as he had mounted the rostrum. Everywhere seemed to spread one huge smile of anticipation across the rows of faces confronting him. Syndercombe stood in silence for a time, then politely raised his hand. The hubbub died to complete stillness.

In a voice as resonant and grave as usual, Syndercombe began: 'Ladies and gentlemen, before the sale starts I have an important and, I fear, disappointing announcement to make. One painting listed in your catalogue has been withdrawn from the sale. You will no longer be able to bid for the *Venus Revealed*, the Velazquez.'

For a moment the silence seemed to sink to an even greater depth of silence; then a hum, which rose almost immediately to a roar of astonishment; all those hundreds of pairs of eyes staring at him with bewilderment, all those jaws dropping. He was aware of the television snouts swivelling on to him, and of the sudden rush of newspapermen towards the exit, where they paused, poised for the telephone but awaiting the explanation.

Several eminent men had risen, waving catalogues at him and voicing protests. The one that Syndercombe first distinguished was a leading dealer from St James's crying in his clear tone, 'But you can't do that, Syndercombe. It's up for auction. How can a firm of your standing countenance such a thing?'

Then the angry, nasal, booming voice of the greatest American dealer of them all: 'We demand an explanation. Why has the Velazquez been withdrawn?'

Another American voice cut in: 'You've brought us thousands of miles, at great expense, to this sale. You can't withdraw the lot we've all come for.'

The greatest American dealer again: 'Mr Syndercombe, why has the Velazquez been withdrawn? If it has been sold privately, prior to auction, I warn you that the gravest consequences will follow for you and your firm.' The crowd was quietening now, accepting him as spokesman. 'Mr Syndercombe, on behalf of my colleagues and myself, I ask for—no, I demand—an answer now. Why has the Velazquez been withdrawn? Has it been sold privately? If it has, we demand to know in what circumstances, and to whom. I am not making any threats—that will be for our legal advisers to consider at leisure. But I am telling you that, for the sake of the standing of your firm and yourself in the world of art transactions, you had better give us an answer now. Why has the Velazquez been withdrawn?'

Syndercombe made a stiff, courteous bow in the American's direction. 'Of course you shall have an answer now. The Velazquez has been withdrawn for reasons over which neither we nor the owner of the painting had any control. It has not been sold prior to auction to any private purchaser. Surely I do not need to assure you that the firm of Crosby's, and I as an individual, would never consent to any such practice, legal or not.

'The Velazquez has been withdrawn, ladies and gentlemen, because it is no longer in our possession.

'The facts have not as yet been fully established, but an investigation by Scotland Yard is already under way. We have to withdraw the painting from this sale because last night, or early this morning—we cannot be sure, as yet, when or how—it was stolen.'

In the riot of noise that, after another moment of silence, broke out in the Great Room, Syndercombe descended from the rostrum and walked without deflection out of the door. He had arranged for one of the younger men to conduct the rest of the sale. He could not have faced that.

As he emerged from the lift to return to his office, Grant came breathlessly to tell him, 'The place is already besieged with reporters. What do we say?'

'Nothing. Tell them there will be no statement from Crosby's on this matter, now or at any other time. And Geoffrey, see that every member of the staff is informed that anybody detected in saying one word to a newspaper or television reporter will be dismissed without notice or compensation. Yes, what is it, Sergeant?'

'Mr Foy asks, sir, if you'll please come at once to the

control room,' said Sergeant Madge. 'It's a matter of urgency.'

Foy was holding a telephone. He proffered it to Syndercombe. 'Will you tell me, sir, whether you recognize the voice speaking on this phone?'

Syndercombe took it. 'Hallo. Who is that?'

'Syndercombe. At last, somebody with some sense! Listen, it's an outrage . . .'

Syndercombe almost dropped the phone. 'Charles! It's Harrison. Where are you, Charles? What in heaven's name have you been doing?'

'Doing? Damn and blast all the devils in hell! I've not been doing anything—I've been done by.'

'Have you got the Velazquez?'

'Have I got the . . .? What's all this about? Are you telling me something has happened to the Velazquez. Syndercombe. Syndercombe. In Satan's name, answer me. What has happened to the Velazquez?'

With a gesture of complete helplessness, beyond speech, Syndercombe handed the phone back to Foy's outstretched hand. Foy took up, 'We can't explain anything on the phone, Mr Harrison. The essential is to get you back to London. Please ask the Inspector to come back on the line. Inspector, please get Mr Harrison here, to Crosby's, by the fastest car you have.' He put down the phone.

'Where is he?' Syndercombe almost shouted, his calm and gravity vanished.

'He's in a police station at Evesham in Worcestershire.'

'What's he doing there? Has he got the picture? Has he been arrested?'

'He hasn't got the picture, and he hasn't been arrested. He has been kidnapped—or so he says.'

'By the police?'

'Of course not. He says that last evening, just as he was preparing to leave his house to come on duty here, there was a ring at the bell. He was alone in the house.

'He answered the door and a man wearing a mask pushed his way quickly into the hall and threatened him with a gun. His hands were tied behind him and his mouth was gagged. He was then made to step into a small van that had been pulled up by his front door.

'The man followed and pinioned him so that he could not move. Then the van drove off. Somebody else was driving. It stopped after a few minutes to let the first man out, then drove all night, only stopping once for the driver to fill up the tank from petrol cans stowed in the rear. Early this morning the driver parked the van, made sure that Mr Harrison was in no danger from his bonds or the gag, and went away.

'About half an hour ago a call from a country phone booth to the Evesham police informed them that a man was tied up in the back of a van parked in a wood behind an orchard on the outskirts of a nearby village. They found Mr Harrison. To verify his story, they came through here. And that's all we know.'

'But I'm completely bewildered,' said Syndercombe. 'You mean it wasn't Charles in here last night with the picture? But he was here. Mr Finch and all the others saw him. He gave a Press conference. The photograph of him in this room is in *The Times* this morning. So what's all this bosh about being kidnapped and taken to Evesham?'

'I think the man in this room last night was not Mr Harrison, but a thief impersonating him—Mr Harrison having been taken out of the way for the night. Since the thieves realized that they had no chance of penetrating Finch's security screen, in order to switch the painting, they used an alternative ploy. They switched the man.'

CHAPTER VII

Frosso knew it was essential for her to stay at the sale rooms all day, much as she wanted to get back to Chelsea and check that there had been no hitch. Chief Superintendent Foy might seem plodding and hesitant, but she had the feeling that, behind the screen of slowness, he was as alert as a squirrel, storing away every tiny circumstance in his memory, in case it should prove later to be any kind of indication. So on that particular day Charles Harrison's secretary must not make any slight move that could attract his attention.

Also, of course, it was valuable to learn as much as she could of what was going on. So she made herself indispensable, organizing sandwiches and drinks for Mr Syndercombe and the policemen, busying in and out of the room. She learned that Charles had been found in the van near Evesham and was on his way back to London; that the van in which he had been driven away had quickly been identified as one stolen in Reading a couple of days earlier; and, by mid-afternoon, that the green van in which the picture had been carried away from the mews had been found abandoned close to Wimbledon Common.

'That was quick of the police,' she said admiringly to the young one, the detective-sergeant.

'Quite an easy trick, miss,' he told her. 'Chances were it had been stolen within forty-eight hours. There was only one green van of small size nicked in that time—from Bishop's Stortford, in Herts. So we had the probable make and registration number, which was circulated to patrols in and around London. Chances were, the chap wouldn't have gone far in it. It wasn't long before a patrol at Wimbledon picked it up.'

'Will it help you to catch the thief?' she asked, wide-eyed.

'Doubt it. I suppose there might be fingerprints, or wool scraping from his clothes which the forensic science people could do something with. But it isn't likely that a clever thief left a visiting card.'

'It's absolutely fascinating to see the way you policemen work.'

He seemed not to have noticed anything ironic in the remark.

When, shortly after three o'clock, Charles arrived back, unshaven, dishevelled from his night's captivity, shaken by the police-car ride to London, her luck was even better. If there were any question of his being suspected of complicity, he declared, he wanted a verbatim record of what was said. 'Frosso, bring your notebook.'

So she sat in on the discussion, taking a shorthand note, as Charles related what had happened to him. It told her little she didn't already know, until Foy asked if he had seen anything of the two men who attacked him, that might enable him to recognize them again.

Charles hesitated. Frosso held her pencil poised on the notebook, waiting.

'Not the one who broke into the house, I don't think,' he said after a pause for recollection. 'He was wearing a sort of carnival mask over his face, like a red-cheeked farmer.'

'You'd have seen something or other,' Foy encouraged him, 'if you think back carefully. His eyes, for instance.'

'I must have seen them through the mask, but I've got no recollection. It wasn't exactly a moment for calm observation. I was damn scared.'

'Was he tall or short, fat or thin?'

'About a couple of inches shorter than I am. That'd

make him about five feet nine. Thin—definitely thin, wiry. He was wearing a boiler suit over whatever he had on, and a workman's cap that covered up most of his hair. I suppose some hair was showing, but I don't remember anything about it.'

'Voice?'

'Ah yes,' said Charles thoughtfully, 'voice. Educated, southern England—probably London. He didn't say much, but enough to tell that. On second thoughts, I'm not so sure about the education. It might have been carefully cultivated—chap got on in the world a bit and deliberately improved the class of his speaking voice.'

Foy sighed. 'Not much to go on.'

'I was being kidnapped, not playing a parlour game.'

'How about the driver of the van?'

'Yes, I saw more of him. It was when he came round to check me over before he left. He had tied a blue silk scarf or handkerchief over the bottom half of his face, but it didn't hide him fully.'

'Don't stop to think. Just say what you can remember, quickly.'

'Youngish, middle-twenties I'd guess. Thuggish face, fair curly hair, thick forehead and thick nose. Rather small eyes—haven't a clue what colour. He was wearing old blue jeans and a thick, rather dirty, high-neck white woollen sweater. His hands were grimed and calloused, like a labourer's.'

'Voice?'

'He didn't speak.'

'Do you think you could pick out his photograph?'

'I might,' agreed Charles dubiously, 'if the lower half of the face in the photograph were covered up.'

'I know it's an imposition, sir, after all you've been through,' said Foy. 'But would you agree to drive along to the Yard now, so that Sergeant Madge can show you a selection of photographs?'

'If it's likely to be of any use.'

'It could be the one lead we really need.'

As Madge took him out, Foy added, 'By the way, Madge, while you're there, show Mr Harrison a selection of the likeliest kind of pistol. You mght be able to tell us, sir, which pistol was used in your house.'

Frosso followed Charles and asked, 'Will you want this transcript today, Mr Harrison? I've been here since rather early this morning, and I'm a bit fagged.'

'No, of course not. Any time tomorrow will do. Cut along now, Frosso. I'll be here in the morning. Phone if you don't feel up to coming.'

'Oh, I'll be here,' she assured him. She gave a little giggle. 'Sounds awful, but it's so terribly exciting—wouldn't miss it for anything.'

She walked to Piccadilly and took the bus. Nobody was watching her, but she understood the importance of not doing anything unusual. It would be part of her self-discipline, not to make the slightest slip or give anything away. For although it was immensely valuable to be at the heart of the enemy camp, it was obviously dangerous. To arouse the smallest suspicion could be fatal.

The shop was shut. When she climbed the stairs, both men were there.

'Everything okay?' she asked.

'Went like a dream,' Sebastian assured her.

Hugh Dell, looking up from the chaise-longue on which he was sitting, asked, 'Anything to tell us from your end?'

'They've got a pretty good idea of what happened. They've traced both vans, and found the green one. Charles is back in London and has gone to the Yard to try to identify the sort of pistol you used, and the driver who took him off. The idiot let Charles get quite a good look at him when he checked him over this morning.'

'I don't think we need worry overmuch,' said Dell. 'It won't matter if he identifies the pistol—a common make. As for the driver, forget him. He doesn't know anything at all about you two and not much about me. He doesn't need to meet me any more. I paid him with a hundred used £1 notes on the spot—been withdrawing small amounts from my bank for some time. By the way,' he added to Sebastian, 'wasn't that a little expense you were going to take care of?'

Sebastian took a bundle of notes from a drawer in his desk and handed them to Dell. 'I've been milking the till gradually too. There are a hundred there. Hadn't you better count them?'

Dell pushed them into his pocket. 'If I didn't trust you that far, I wouldn't be here.'

Sebastian grinned. 'Frosso, my pet, there's a bottle of Mumm Cordon Rouge in the fridge.'

She brought out the bottle for Sebastian to uncork. Over the first glass he nodded to her. 'Here's to the onlie begetter.'

'I'll drink to that,' said Dell. 'As neat a bit of staff work as ever I've seen. The touch I enjoyed most was getting the security men to phone you this morning telling you to come to the office—getting them, in fact, to tip you off that Sebastian was just starting out for George Street with the picture, so that you could phone me to get the van in position in the mews before I smashed the telephone in the booth to look like normal vandalism. That was brilliant criminal planning. Have you had much practice?'

'My maiden effort.'

'You must persevere. You have unusual talent.'

She dropped him a mock curtsey. 'Shall I ever have such inspiration again?' she wondered. 'There was I that morning, taking dictation from Charles, and

Charles was nattering on about his Velazquez and the lolly it'd make, and it suddenly came to me that, if Sebastian had that shaped moustache, and somewhat different-coloured hair, there was a marked resemblance between them. And I found myself fancying that, as Sebastian is an actor of sorts . . .'

'Of sorts?' he cried in pretended rage. 'You dare say that, after my star performance?'

'Well, I found myself fancying that he could easily impersonate Charles Harrison. Of course, he couldn't have kept it up with anybody who knew Charles at all well. But he wouldn't have to. For I knew all about the tradition of guarding a masterpiece on the night before the sale. And at that moment . . .'

She looked at Hugh Dell expectantly.

'It came to you whole, just like that,' he said.

'Yes. You understand. Is it always like that?'

He laughed. 'Very rarely.'

'I did see it whole. It would be necessary to get Charles out of the way for one night, which meant getting help from somebody like you. Then Sebastian could walk in as Charles. The only people he would have to fool were a few security men who had met Charles only once. He could easily stage the attack on himself, scratch the back of the frame to make out it had been tampered with, swear as an expert it was a forgery, there had been a switch, and take it out of the building under their noses. I tell you, I did see it absolutely whole, just like that.' She paused, and added, almost shyly, 'It was like touching an electric wire.'

Dell nodded. 'I know the feeling.'

'The only thing I didn't see was that there would be a security man with Sebastian when he took the picture off. But he saw that at once, and that the man would have to be dealt with and that he couldn't do it on his own. But it didn't really add to the problem. We had to have you anyway overnight, so it made no more difference if we also had to have you in the morning.'

Sebastian, sipping happily, protested that the essence of success was not Hugh, but himself. Look how he had trained for the part. 'Frosso brought home some of Harrison's tapes on which he'd dictated letters, and I played them back and back until I could imitate his voice almost exactly. Then she turned up some colour photographs of him that had been taken fairly recently for some publicity thing. She even got a few hairs off the collar of his jacket; he has a little dandruff, luckily. Well then, there's this hair dye that washes off quite easily afterwards, as you can see—I washed it off directly I got back. There wasn't time to grow enough moustache, but I could fix one on quite easily, and the whole appearance, plus the voice, would be good enough to fool anybody who had met Harrison only once or twice. As it was. It went like a dream. There was only one moment when I had a touch of panic. That was when the silly old fool of a security man said I'd have to leave the picture where it was, to be tested for fingerprints. But I persuaded him that the frame would be enough.'

Dell asked whether he had left his own prints on the frame, and Sebastian admitted that he had. He had to get the canvas out of the back. But what did it matter? Nobody had his fingerprints, and there were probably several sets on the frame anyway—the porters' and all that. It couldn't be important.

'Not unless they arrest you,' agreed Dell drily.

'Come on, now. How can they connect it with me?'

'There is just the business of getting the ransom, which can be a lot trickier than getting the picture.'

'You needn't worry about that,' said Frosso quickly.

'We shan't ask you to take any part in that. Your risks are over.'

He smiled gently. 'But my tongue will be hanging out until you have safely got the money. How much are you going to ask?'

'Haven't decided yet,' replied Sebastian uneasily.

'Ah well, it'll be in the newspapers in good time,' said Dell, rising. 'Might even tempt me to ask you for a bigger cut.'

'Now, look here Hugh, let's have this straight now. You undertook to do your part of the job for a certain sum. You'll get that sum, as promised.'

'Provided you get the ransom.'

'How can we fail? We've got the picture.'

'Where is it, by the way?'

'Somewhere quite safe, where it won't be found,' Sebastian assured him. 'I'm the only one who knows. Later on I shall tell Frosso, as a precaution, if I have to put myself at risk. It would be better for you not to know. We're not going to double-cross you.'

'I'm sure you're not,' the other pleasantly replied.

'You can be quite sure, because I very well know that, if I did, you'd cut my throat.'

Dell laughed. 'There are subtler ways.'

When he had gone, Sebastian gleefully tipped the rest of the champagne into his glass; Frosso refused any more. Was she still worrying about Dell? he asked. Forget it. Old Hugh was okay. Balancing his glass in one hand, he caught hold of her with the other and urged her towards the bedroom. 'We've had a wonderful day. Let's crown it with a wonderful night.'

She protested that she was exhausted, but he would hear none of that. So she got into bed with him, but disliking it, listless. Exhaustion, she thought, was not the reason. Could the reason be that this sensation was so inferior to the other? Or that Sebastian, in his cups, became something of a clown of whom she was tiring? But then, perhaps after all it was merely exhaustion. Anyway, it did not matter. He was too tipsy to notice her lack of response.

CHAPTER VIII

At his desk in Sawdon House, Bullen was scanning with amusement the headlines of the morning papers. 'The best is undoubtedly RAPE OF VENUS,' he remarked to Rose. 'That's the *Mirror* of course. I don't give any marks to the *Telegraph*'s THE GREAT PAINT ROBBERY. The *Telegraph* usually does better than that. *The Times* scores with VELAZQUEZ MASTERPIECE STOLEN FROM LOCKED AND GUARDED ROOM.'

Rose looked up from the typed list on her desk. 'We were checking this inventory of bed-linen with the accounts.'

He smiled at her, reluctantly dropping the newspapers on the floor. 'Quite right. But they are rather absorbing. They have the whole story, practically.'

'Only because you gave it to them, in spite of Mr Grant and police advice.'

'Adds to the gaiety of the nation.'

Directly the news of the robbery broke at Crosby's, reporters had rushed at him. He let them all in. He had the habit of never turning anybody away. And he told them all he knew of the robbery. 'Crosby's aren't going to approve of this,' he told them genially. 'Nor are the police. I've been told not to talk. So don't overdo it, please.'

One of them assured him, 'You couldn't over-write this one.'

'After all, Sir David,' said another, 'it's your picture, not theirs.'

'Oh no. It was given to the Sawdon Trust. Which means it really belongs to all the homeless families we can cram into our hostels this year, next year, ever after—until England becomes a country where every man can expect a roof for his wife and children. That's why I hope that whoever took the painting will give it back. After all, it's of no value to the thief.'

'Why do you think it was taken?'

'I've no idea. I'm told the picture is so well publicized that it couldn't be sold illegally anywhere in the world. So why anybody wants to steal it . . . On that question, gentlemen, I'm sure your imaginations are more fertile than mine.'

As the morning papers showed, they were.

Rose resumed reading aloud the linen list, so that he could check. The phone went. 'Damn,' she muttered.

'Who is that? Oh yes, of course, Superintendent. Come along whenever you like.' To Rose he said, 'The Yard man. He's coming to see us.'

Without comment, Rose continued reading down the list of sheets and towels, Bullen grunting assent as he checked each item. But in a few minutes the door opened. A bedraggled woman stood there, with two small bedraggled girls. Rose stopped reading, without impatience. She was used to this.

'Fellow downstairs said to come up,' began the woman. 'Is it all right?'

'Of course. We don't believe in locked doors. Indeed,' he smiled at her, 'we've just had a perfect example of how useless they are. Come in. You are . . .?'

'Mrs Symes—Mary Symes. These are my two—Kathleen and Grace.'

'Well now, Mrs Symes . . .'

It was the usual story—evicted from a furnished

room. The magistrate gave them security for three months, and now that was up. All the local authority could offer was hostels—and that meant that Len, her husband, must go to one, and she take the children to another, splitting up.

'We've no accommodation,' Rose warned him in a low voice.

'Then we'll have to find some. This is Miss Pearson, who looks after us all, and performs about six miracles every day. Is Len working in London? Then it'll have to be here, in Sawdon House. It'll be cramped. But we'll do what we can to find you somewhere to live as soon as possible, so you won't have to stay here long, I hope—and so does Miss Pearson hope!'

The door opened again. 'Oh, sorry. I was told to come up,' said Foy. 'Didn't know you were engaged.'

'Come in, Mr Foy. This goes on all the time. I suppose you've come to scold me for talking to the newspapers.'

'That was one of the things I had in mind, sir.'

'Sorry. But it seemed to me the thief must be some sort of crank, rather like myself. So I wanted him to get the message that the *Venus Revealed* is not just an Old Master painting—it's a touch of hope for thousands of people who are in trouble. The best way to get this message to him seemed to be the newspapers and television, and they've published just what I wanted them to. I think there's a good chance it might bring the picture back to us quickly.'

Foy hesitated. 'Well, let's hope you're right.'

'After all, Mr Foy, whoever stole it didn't do it for personal gain. There can be no gain. So he's a man of unstable mind—like me—and he might well be moved by, for instance, Mrs Symes here, and Kathleen and Grace. Just tell this man what you were telling me, Mrs Symes.'

Foy listened uneasily. So there was trouble in the world. Of course there was. But he was a criminal investigator, not a missionary. Rose Pearson, he saw with gratitude, understood his embarrassment and, when the woman had finished, led her and the two children away.

'There were other things you wanted to mention?' asked Bullen.

'Yes, Sir David. I admit frankly that I don't yet understand the motive for this robbery. But I don't think it was the work of an eccentric, or a crank. It was far too skilful and subtle for that. I almost said professional, but there I think I should have been wrong. It hasn't got the stamp of a professional criminal. It seems more like—how shall I say?—a brilliant amateur. But I'm sure the purpose behind it is a serious one. It may most likely be something not connected at all with you, or your family, or the Sawdon Trust and the work you are doing. But there's a chance that it might be. If you had, for instance, some particular enemy . . .'

Bullen was no longer smiling. 'All mankind should be my enemy, Mr Foy. There might be some individual, probably from Germany but possibly from France, who has waited all these years for the ideal way of getting even. But it seems far-fetched. The war ended more than a quarter of a century ago.'

'I was thinking,' said Foy, 'of a rather more personal enemy. For example—not that I'm suggesting anything —you have an heir, a cousin I believe. It could be possible that the heir is angered at the way the family money and possessions are going to the charitable causes you serve. So he decides to prevent the sale of the most valuable of all, and will keep it safe until the inheritance is his.'

'Cousin Simon? I suppose it's just possible. He certainly does moan about the family money. But since the estate isn't entailed, there's nothing he can do about it—unless, as you say, it was he who took the Velazquez. Not that it would do him any good. I gave the painting by deed of gift to the Sawdon Trust months ago, so Simon couldn't inherit it. He might not know that. But it sounds a bit too much of an operation for him, he's not particularly bright. You can check if you wish. He lives in Paris. I forget his address, but I'll get Rose to look it up and phone it to you.'

'Thank you, sir. And any other possible enemy—if that's the way to put it—who occurs to you. If you'd just mention it to me, quite between ourselves.'

'I'll see how many enemies I can think of.'

Getting up to go, Foy added, 'There's only one other point, a real long-shot. With all this publicity you're certainly going to get contacts, probably by phone, from several madmen—cranks, as you put it. It'll be a thousand to one that any caller has anything at all to do with it. Every publicized crime produces a small crop of publicity-seeking or just plain crazy confessors to it. Nevertheless we can't let even the slightest chance slip. If you do get anything like that, try to find out as much as you can about the caller, and always let my office know at once.'

Bullen nodded, reaching for the phone which had started to ring. He listened, a sad look in his eyes; through the phone a man's guttural voice was pouring obscenities. Bullen silently handed the receiver to Foy, who listened for a moment, clicked his tongue sympathetically and hung up.

'You're bound to get some of that too. It's that headline, "Rape of Venus", that will have triggered them off. Try to prevent any women on your staff from picking up the phone first for a few days. If it gets too bad, we can have the line intercepted.'

When Rose returned, Bullen told her that, for the

next few days, she was not to pick up the phone; he himself would take all the calls. 'There will be some poor, perverted wretches ringing up to relieve themselves by shouting obscenities down the phone. We've had one already. It doesn't worry me in the least—but it would worry me a lot if you or any of the girls working here were subjected to it. Foy says it'll last probably only a few days.'

So it was Bullen himself who answered the call at 7.30 that evening. First came the pips, so it was from a callbox. Then a voice with a slight north-country whine murmured: 'We've got your picture, Sir David. You can have it back, if you want—at a price.'

'I don't quite understand . . .'

'We have the Velazquez. It is safe and undamaged. No, don't say anything. I'm not staying long on this line. And it'd be pointless for you to try to get the call traced. In fact, if you say anything at all to the police, neither you nor anybody else will see the painting again. It will be destroyed. But if you do as I say, you will get it back safely. The price for its return is a quarter of a million pounds. You can then sell it for two million, and have a million and three quarters to spend on your hostels.'

Bullen said, with a short laugh, 'That's absurd. I don't possess a quarter of a million pounds.'

'Think it over, Sir David. You'll quickly see how you can raise the money. In a couple of days, when I'm sure you're not bringing in the police, I'll be in touch with you again, to tell you how to proceed.'

'There have been several madmen on this phone today,' said Bullen. 'What possible reason can I have for thinking that you aren't another, but really have the painting?'

'Tomorrow you'll get a plain envelope through the post, marked personal, with the number 8 written on the back flap. It will contain the proof.'

The phone clicked and the dialling tone started up with its usual soft purr.

After supper he told Rose of the phone call. 'It may be just another crank. But I had an odd feeling that it isn't. The voice on the phone was assumed. He was trying to give it a sort of basic scowse, as though he'd lived in Liverpool as a youth, and come away to London, never totally losing the accent. It wasn't quite genuine—we get enough Liverpudlians in Sawdon for me to be fairly sure of that. A crank wouldn't try to fake an accent, there'd be no reason. But if it were the real chap, there could be a very strong one. We assumed too readily that there could be no financial gain from the theft of the *Venus*, because it couldn't be sold to anybody. But it can be, Rose. It can be sold back to me. Somehow one thinks of kidnapping as always involving a person. But why not an object, if valuable enough? That call could be genuine.'

'You'll know by tomorrow, since he promised proof in the post. Have you told the police?'

'Not yet.'

'Why not?'

'We have different objectives. I want to get the picture back by any means and I don't give a damn about catching and punishing the thieves. The police want to recover the painting, of course, but primarily they want to catch the thieves. From their point of view, and from the point of view of the public good, no doubt they're right. But not from mine. We all know what it will mean to Sawdon if we can get it back and sell it.'

'You want my opinion?' asked Rose. 'I think you have to tell the police. But wait until tomorrow's post to make sure it isn't just a madman.'

Bullen nodded. 'That's reasonable.'

The mail was brought up to his desk after breakfast.

Rose went upstairs with him. He flicked through the neat pile of envelopes. Then his fingers stopped and he drew one out, extending it to show her. It was a plain, cheap manila envelope. The address was written in capital letters, drawn with the broad black strokes of a felt pen. Bullen turned the envelope over. On the back flap was written the numeral 8.

Carefully he slit the envelope with a paperknife, peered inside, then reached for a clean sheet of blotting paper on to which he tipped the contents—a small piece of canvas painted on the front.

'Proof?' queried Rose. 'It could be anything.'

Bullen shook his head. From a drawer in his desk he pulled out the issue of *Apollo* which contained a reproduction of the *Venus Revealed*, the best that had been published. 'Here in this bottom corner right at the edge you can see the small draping of lace across the bed, and the fringe of tassel of a silk cord.' Carefully he laid the small scrap of canvas by the side of the print. 'It's only a reproduction, and on a much smaller scale. But do you doubt that these indications on the scrap of canvas are part of the pattern just here in the painting?'

'Any forger could have done that,' she objected.

'Granted. But that rules out the crank or madman. Either this is a forged scrap of canvas, which can only mean there's a criminal trying to con a ransom out of us by pretending to have the painting, or it's genuine, and comes from the thief. My bet's the thief.'

Rose pointed out that the fact could be determined. There was enough paint and canvas for the Frobisher laboratory to say for sure whether they came from the Velazquez or not.

'But that means going to the police,' objected Bullen. 'I can't turn up at the Institute, or the National Gallery, to ask them to date a scrap of canvas, without making it plain that I'm in touch with the thief.'

'Then that seems to settle it. Tell the police.'

'The threat was that, if I did, the painting would be destroyed.'

'It's an obvious threat, David. But they wouldn't carry it out. If they did, they'd destroy their whole purpose. Anyway, they couldn't know whether you'd informed the police or not.'

After a pause, Bullen nodded, reached for the phone and dialled the number he had been given. 'Chief Superintendent Foy, please. Ah, is that you speaking? I think I may be in touch with the thief of the painting. Or rather, not the thief—the kidnapper.'

Foy was silent for a moment. Then he drew in a deep breath. 'For a ransom, Sir David?'

'For a ransom of a quarter of a million pounds.'

He told him briefly of the phone call, the scrap of canvas, the threat if the police were brought in.

'Essential there should be no hint of that,' Foy agreed. 'I shan't come near you today. Tomorrow we'll call a meeting at Crosby's. Don't say anything to anyone there about this contact but, before we break up, slip the envelope and the piece of canvas to me. I'll get it vetted in strict secrecy. If it's genuine, I'll telephone you to say so. Then we wait for the next call from the man with the phoney scowse accent. I'm going to have a tap put on your line to Sawdon House—I take it you don't object.'

'Can't say I like the idea,' replied Bullen uneasily. 'But no, I suppose I don't object.'

When he had rung off, he turned to Rose, saying, 'Our phone's going to be tapped by the police. Foy will get the canvas tested. I've an unhappy feeling that we're going the right way to catch the thieves, and the wrong way to get the painting back. Please God I'm wrong.'

CHAPTER IX

The room over the shop stank of cigarette smoke. That was one of the signs that worried Frosso. Sebastian was now lighting one from another, sometimes finding himself with one between his lips while another smouldered in the ashtray beside his chair—at which he laughed nervously.

Then there were sudden spurts of irritability. Then, inevitably, reefers. She protested that he was a fool to take that sort of risk at that time, but he shook her hand from his arm and went down to the shop, rummaging among the junk, as though that might distract him.

He was still down there when Hugh Dell came up the stairs to the living-room. Frosso hesitated for a moment, then told him, 'Sebastian's started to drug.'

Dell regarded her in silence. But when Sebastian came upstairs, Dell said quietly, 'Sebastian, I want all the pot you've got.'

'What the devil's it got to do with you?'

'Too big a risk. For one thing, you'll dull your wits, just when you need them. For another, it could lead to a police search here.'

'What of it? There's nothing here for them to find.'

'I still want that pot. I'm not having you balls the thing up, just because you're losing your nerve.'

'You mind your own bloody business. I'm running this show.'

'I've a stake in it,' said Dell, 'which I don't intend to lose.'

She thought Sebastian would flare up again, but instead he suddenly shrugged, smiled weakly and admitted, 'Sorry. It's the waiting that gets me. I'll not touch it again.'

'Better give it to me, to be sure.'

'I've told you,' repeated Sebastian irritably, 'I'll not touch it again.'

Dell stayed only briefly. Just before he went, he looked inquiringly to Frosso. After a moment's pause, she told him, 'In that china potpourri jar on the top shelf.'

Without a word, Dell picked up the jar and took it with him.

When he had gone, Frosso put her arms round Sebastian. 'It makes sense, after all.'

'I suppose so,' he muttered. 'But we're going to have to watch that bastard. If he knew where the painting was . . .'

'Where is it?'

'You'd better not know either until you have to. And the sooner that is, the better. I tell you, Frosso, this waiting is knifing me. Did you get any hint at your place today?'

She shook her head. 'They called a meeting—the partners, the police, the security men and Bullen. Charles was in it too. By what he said afterwards, there was nothing special to it—just working carefully over the ground again to see if they'd missed anything. It did no good, Charles said, the police still haven't got any idea. Which looks as though Bullen is playing along with us so far.'

'We ought to move again,' murmured Sebastian uneasily, almost to himself. 'The longer we wait, the more chances of something being discovered.'

'There's nothing they could discover, until we move again. We've got to be as sure as we can be, before we do. Give it another twenty-four hours.'

Fumbling for a cigarette from a half-crushed packet,

he grudgingly agreed.

Next evening Dell was there again. 'You'd better give the man another call.'

'Suppose they've tapped his line.'

'Of course they have,' said Dell briskly, almost contemptuously. 'You must have made allowance for that.'

'The difficulty is that, wherever I call from, if they've tapped Bullen's line they can get a police car to me in a couple of minutes.'

'Difficult, yes,' agreed Dell, slightly smiling. 'But you're running the show. You'll find a way, no doubt.'

'All right, Hugh,' said Frosso, 'you're the professional. Tell the amateurs how to do it.'

Dell glanced at Sebastian, who nodded sullenly.

'You make Bullen use another line that the police haven't tapped. When you ring him from your first callbox, you tell him to go straight to the public callbox down the street—there'll be one nearby. The monitor in at the Yard will hear that, so he'll hook up as quickly as he can to that callbox number; it'll take him quite a little while.

'But when Bullen gets there, he finds a note, which I've left for him the moment I see him coming. This directs him to go by Underground to some distant station and wait for a call at a specified public callbox there, at a given time, which allows him only just sufficient margin to get there, and none to start alerting the police. In any case, I'll be around, watching him. If he tries anything on, I warn you, and you drop the operation for that night. But if all goes well—I accompany him on the Underground as an additional precaution—then you ring him from some other callbox and you can take as long as you like, there isn't a chance of the police latching on to it.'

'Tomorrow?' asked Frosso.
'Yes, we can be ready by then.'

The evening was nearly dark when Bullen got the second call. 'This is me again, Sir David. I take it you still want to get your picture back.' The same scowse voice; Bullen was surer than ever that the accent was faked. 'Very well then. Go to the public telephone kiosk near the railway bridge over Latchmere Road. Do you know it?'

'I'll find it.'

'I'll ring you there.'

The click, the purring tone.

Rose, who had been standing by the window, asked, 'Do you know you're being tailed? There's a man in the shadow on the far side of the road.'

'Police?'

'I should think so. He seems to be in contact with somebody just round the corner, probably a car.'

'I'll use the back alley.'

Bullen hurried down to the back entrance to Sawdon House, which opened into the alley. A couple of guests coming up the stairs greeted him, and he them; but few others noticed him, there was a sing-song in the main room. The alley led to a side street not far from Latchmere Road. He at once saw the phone booth which he must have passed a score of times without noticing.

Directly he stepped into the booth he saw the note, on cheap lined paper, with his name at the top. The same broad capitals written in black with a felt pen. 'Take the Tube, Clapham North to Tooting Bec. Will ring second booth outside station at 10.25.'

Bullen looked at his watch. That gave him about twenty-five minutes. He could just do it, if he had luck with the trains. He started at a fast walk towards Lavender Hill. Luckily, as he came out by Clapham Common, he picked up a taxi. That saved him a good five minutes; which was as well, for there was a four-minute wait for the next southbound train.

The lights of Balham High Road were flaring when he came up from the Tube. Evening crowds were flowing up and down, girls in pairs, elderly men in and out of the pubs, a picturesque sprinkling of Negroes, young couples, arms entwined, turning south towards the bushes and solitudes of the common, music streaming from a jukebox in an amusement arcade, the smell of frying fish. Bullen got into the second phone booth from the station entrance with a couple of minutes to spare. He pretended to search for a number in the grimed, torn directory.

The phone rang. 'Hallo.'

'Hallo, Sir David. Glad you made it. Continue to co-operate and you'll get your picture back. Now listen. I'm not going to say anything twice, and I won't be long on this line. Have you made arrangements to get the money?'

'No. But I probably can.'

'There are American dealers still in London?'

'Yes, that's the gist of it.'

'It must be in used £5 and £1 notes that'll go into two suitcases. How you get the notes is your problem. You've got until next Tuesday. Either on that day, or some day later, I'll phone you again at Sawdon House with instructions. If you try to bring in the police, the picture will be destroyed.'

'Never mind about the police,' said Bullen firmly. 'I want the painting—and I don't give a damn about catching you. But you don't get the money until I'm sure I get the painting. If I turn up with the money at whatever rendezvous you appoint, you must turn up at the same time with the picture. I shall have an expert with me who will know whether it's the genuine Velazquez or not.'

'You're in no position to set conditions, Sir David.'

'Nevertheless, those are the conditions. If you don't accept them, you don't get the money and I go straight to Scotland Yard with what information I can give them.'

The click, and the gentle purring of the disconnected line.

An empty taxi came by. Bullen took it back to Sawdon House. He saw with amusement that the policeman was still standing in the shadows opposite and was obviously startled to see him on the street.

Upstairs he dialled the number at the Yard that Foy had given him, Foy's own desk number.

'The boss has gone home, Sir David. This is Sergeant Madge. I'm keeping night watch. Any developments, sir?'

'Yes, but they'll keep till morning. Ask Mr Foy to ring me directly he gets in. And Sergeant, ask him to call off the man who is watching me.'

'Is there one, sir?' asked Madge innocently. 'I didn't know. I'll tell the Super what you say, Sir David.'

Frosso spent most of the evening, while the two men were away, in the seat by the window, from which she had a distant view of the King's Road parade, the unkempt men with their straggling hair and the obedient girls so solemn in their gaiety, seeming to grow even more bizarre, more dramatic, like a scroll of quaint figures unrolling across a toy theatre, a peepshow, as the evening darkened and the lights of the restaurants and shops came up.

She had once thought that the Chelsea thing was all that she wanted while she was still young; and when she would no longer be young, what would anything matter? But the sensations from which she had hoped most—the succession of men, the solaces of a drug, the assertion of freedom from any restraint, even the one lesbian adventure into which she had wandered from curiosity but had not liked—all these had already dulled.

Would the same happen to the keenest which she had now discovered, the exquisitely unexpected stimulant of crime? Would it degenerate into ordinary hopes and fears—diminishing hopes of triumph, oppressive fears of punishment?

She expected so. Already the sharp excitement of stealing the painting had lessened into the cautious, probably long-drawn-out, perhaps tedious operation of getting the ransom money. She recalled what she could remember of newspaper accounts of kidnappings. Always the manoeuvring for the ransom on the one side, and the release of the kidnapped on the other, was lengthy, slow. But in all those cases a human life was at risk; so the police moved with extreme care, almost with trepidation. There would presumably be no such hindrance to their actions when all that was at risk was a painted piece of canvas, no matter how valuable.

So perhaps, after all, it would be punishment. She admitted that she had not, as yet, truly considered it. Prison. What would it be like? Was it even possible that it might be an experience to be cherished? There were said to be enchanting pleasures in masochism.

She roused herself to reach for another cigarette, telling herself that, in the event, there would be no prison—not now that they had Hugh.

Without him, Sebastian could never have pulled it off; she realized that now. Without Hugh's efficiency in removing Charles for that one night, and coping with the security man in the mews, Sebastian would have floundered into failure. Without Hugh, they could not have hoped to win the game of wits which must be played before the ransom could be seized.

Inevitably, bit by bit, Hugh would assume control, take command. She hoped that Sebastian would be intelligent enough to pretend not to notice it. But inevitably Hugh would demand a much greater share of the ransom. That could well be where the quarrel would come; and a quarrel amongst themselves was the worst risk they could run. It would be better to precipitate it, in the hope that it could be patched up, resolved, because of their common danger.

She had the opportunity almost immediately, for Hugh Dell was the first of the two to get back to the flat; it must be some time before Sebastian returned because he had gone to an outlying northern suburb of London to make his phone calls.

'Did it go all right, Hugh?'

'We shan't know for sure until Sebastian gets back. But he made contact. I could see Bullen talking in the phone booth at Tooting Bec.'

Frosso offered him a scotch, but he shook his head. 'Coffee.'

She filled the percolator and switched it on, getting out a couple of cups on a tray, setting them on the little inlaid table between them. She sat looking at him. There was almost no indication in his trim, sedate appearance of a man of violence; unless it were the unusual paleness of his grey eyes. She wondered what he would be like in bed. Experienced, of course, and probably not in the least gentle. She smiled a little at the thought; the enjoyments of masochism.

She waited until they had coffee in their cups before asking him, with deliberate abruptness, 'You're going to want more than the cut you've been offered, aren't you?'

Now he was smiling. 'Of course. A share, not a fee. You saw that from the start, I'm sure. I doubt whether

Sebastian sees it yet.'

'The worst danger is that we should fall out amongst ourselves.'

'It's a danger, but not the worst. It's not even much of a danger. Neither you nor Sebastian has a hope of collecting the ransom if you are left on your own. If I take control, I believe we can get it. You know that as well as I do, even if Sebastian doesn't see it yet. So, quarrel or no, you can't do without me. I'm leading from strength.'

'But Sebastian holds the trump. He's the only one who knows where the painting is.'

Dell gave her another slow smile. 'Perhaps that could be remedied.' At the way he said that, and the look in his pale eyes, she felt a sudden shiver run through her nerves, almost a quiver of anticipation.

She looked out of the window. 'Sebastian's just coming now,' she said. 'I think we ought to talk of a revision of terms straight away, instead of having it smouldering in the background. It's true that we can't do without you. It's equally true that we're all in it together, and in some ways you can't do without us. So let's be open about it. That way we shall avoid the quarrel which, I still think, is our worst danger.'

'You're probably right,' he said. 'You're an interesting woman.'

Sebastian came up jubilant. 'Everything went fine. No snags.'

'Drink?' she asked.

'Gin. Yes, it was quite smooth. The timing was perfect. No sign of police interference.'

'There might have been,' said Dell.

'How do you mean?'

'They had a tail on Bullen. Luckily he must have seen it. He used the back alley, where I was watching—

nearly bumped into me. I had only just time to nip round and leave the note in the phone booth before he got there.'

Sebastian held out his glass to Frosso for another gin. He was scared, she could see that. If it scared him merely to hear of a risk that had not materialized, what could be expected of him when the action started? She began to understand what Hugh had meant when he said a quarrel between them was not the worst danger. The worst was that they had to depend in some ways on Sebastian, who might crack.

He had recovered himself and was reporting on the phone talk with Bullen. 'So you see,' he concluded, 'I think he'll co-operate. And I don't think he has gone to the police. He doesn't give a damn for crime and punishment—he as good as said so. All he cares about is getting the painting back, to sell for his sickening charities. He insists, though, on having his expert with him when we hand over the painting. Is that feasible?'

'That depends,' answered Dell reflectively. 'I haven't quite made up my mind just what the ransom procedure ought to be.'

Frosso could see Sebastian prickling. 'Perhaps you'll be good enough to tell us about it when you have.'

So then she cut in. 'Sebastian, you're not going to like what I'm going to say now. But we've got to be realistic. You were brilliant in impersonating Charles and getting hold of the picture—don't you agree, Hugh?'

Dell nodded. 'Took a hell of a lot of nerve. Nobody could have done a better job.'

'But, Sebastian, that was a role, something like a part in a play—something you're skilled at and have been trained for. The rest of the job isn't. It's going to be a very tricky, perhaps in the end violent operation, even if the police are kept out of it. All this contacting part you're doing splendidly. But when it comes to the actual job of getting the ransom and passing over the painting, without getting us all caught, it's going to be beyond you. I'm being absolutely frank.'

'So?'

'So we should admit our limitations—admit that we took on more than you and I can handle. I'll make one admission. I thought it was a mistake to take Hugh into it. Now I know it was the move that is most likely to win for us.'

Sebastian's voice was slightly higher in pitch, the indication of his anger. 'Why did you think it was a mistake?'

'You know very well. I thought he was too intelligent, and that the cut you offered him was too high, so that it alerted him to the sort of pay-off we ourselves were expecting. I thought it would be better to hire a thug for the tough job that night. Because it was obvious that, if we let Hugh in on it, he would want to take a much greater share of the operation—and of the profits.'

'As I do,' said Dell.

Sebastian continued to stare morosely at Frosso. 'And you think we should give it to him?'

'I don't think we have any alternative. We can't get the ransom without help from somebody of his kind. It makes sense to accept him.'

'Besides,' said Dell smoothly, 'you couldn't get rid of me. Not now.'

'Why are you so sure we couldn't get the ransom by ourselves,' persisted Sebastian.

'Because of you,' she told him bluntly. 'You're not the right man for the job.'

In an amiable tone, Dell put in, 'Look here, Sebastian, every man has his limitations. Even if I'd been the right size and shape, I couldn't have done what you did on the night we got the painting. I should have cracked and given myself away.

'But the negotiations for the ransom, and the actual collection of the money, are going to need my sort of temperament, not yours. For one thing, you haven't the necessary pessimism. You said just now that you don't think Bullen has gone to the police. Your optimism may be well founded. But suppose he has. It's something we can't be sure about until the crunch comes.

'We ought to assume the worst. You would plan on the assumption that we've only got Bullen to cope with. My assumption would be that we were walking into a police trap. If I were wrong, we'd have an easier time than we planned for. But if you were wrong, we'd almost certainly be nabbed. Because, if the police are in on it, there are going to be moments when we have to take instant decisions and act on them quickly. I've had a good deal of experience of that kind of situation. I don't suppose you've had any.'

While he was talking Frosso grew surer that Sebastian would concede. Partly because he knew that Hugh was right. Partly because at bottom he was thoroughly scared; and knew that, if it came to a crisis, he would be paralysed, helpless. But mostly, she realized, because Sebastian longed to rid himself of the responsibility. He wanted to be told what to do—the born subordinate. Whereas Hugh Dell was the man who automatically gave orders. In any enterprise in which these two were engaged, Hugh would inevitably take control before the real action started, and Sebastian would thankfully sink back into obedience.

In fact he was intelligent enough to see that now. 'What share do you want?' he asked.

'One-third, since there are three of us.'

'At what point will you suddenly demand one-half?'

Dell shrugged. 'Silly question. If I really intended to do that, I shouldn't tell you now. You'll just have to trust me, as I have to trust you. After all, you have the painting. We have to accept each other as partners, without guarantees.'

Pouring himself another gin, Sebastian laughed. 'In a moment you'll be telling me about honour among thieves.'

'The point is,' came in Frosso, 'do we accept? I do.'

'I suppose so,' muttered Sebastian. To Dell he added, 'But if you take one-third of the proceeds, you should stand one-third of the costs. So you owe me £33.33—one-third of the money I gave you for the man who drove the van to Evesham.'

Dell smiled, reached for his wallet, counted out six £5 and three £1 notes, added 33p from the loose change in his pocket and handed the sum to Sebastian, who accepted it cheerfully, remarking, 'Two sides to every coin. Now, what's your plan?'

'I want more time before we discuss it. But we ought to take one precaution straight away. Frosso, how much is known at Crosby's about where you are living?'

'Nothing. I don't discuss my private life.'

'Have they this address?'

'No. I didn't tell them when I moved in here. All I did was change the phone number they had for me on the pad in Charles's desk, and on the switchboard.'

'What is all this?' demanded Sebastian.

'It's dangerous. If any slightest suspicion should arise at Crosby's, they have the phone number of our headquarters.'

'But what sort of suspicion could arise?' she asked.

'Who knows? A moment of carelessness—oh, it's possible for anyone. It needn't even be that. Suppose the Yard man suspects it was an inside job, and starts looking into backgrounds. Can you imagine the sort of suspicions that would arise if he found himself here?'

Sebastian was convinced, she saw that. It was frightening enough to convince him instantly.

'How long have you lived here?' asked Dell.

'Only a couple of months.' And perhaps, the thought came to her, a couple of months was enough. To start with it had been amusing. A journalist, a minor art critic, had introduced Sebastian at some dull party, and Sebastian had been caustic, witty, even funny. The whole affair had been on that sort of level—amusing, civilized and, in bed, gratifying. Sebastian was more efficient in bed than his appearance and his manner promised. She did not regret it. But neither would she regret ending it.

She realized that Hugh was asking her something. 'Hmm?' she queried.

'I said can you, if you move, erase all trace of this phone number from the records at Crosby's?'

'Yes, easily.'

'If you put a new number on the lists in its place, would anybody be likely to realize that it was a different number?'

'Shouldn't think so. I've been rung here only a couple of times, and the girls on the switchboard are always changing. But where would I live, then? Share-a-flat?'

Dell smiled. 'In this country I'm a respectable citizen. I own a little property company—bought it with what I brought back from Africa. The company has a small block of flats in Fulham—nothing grand.' He took a card from his wallet and handed it to her. 'These are our letting agents. The office is close to the Broadway. I'll tell them in the morning that I've met a girl who would like to take the single flat in the block in Barclay Road.'

'Can I afford the rent?'

'For a friend of mine, there is no rent.'

'Oh, Mr Dell,' she mocked him, 'are there any strings?'

'No strings, Miss Teague. Strictly attention to our partnership business.'

Frosso sighed. 'How disappointing!'

Then she caught the look that Sebastian suddenly turned on Hugh. She would have expected him to be, if anything, only amused at that kind of remark; it had certainly not occurred to her that he would be malevolent.

CHAPTER X

Francis Foy was angry. With him, anger never showed. His voice, his gaze, his demeanour were as calm as always; except, perhaps, for an occasional mutter of irritation.

The cause was the report on his desk, when he arrived in the morning, from the man detailed to watch Sir David Bullen; that he had somehow got out of the building without being observed.

Foy's temper was not improved when he rang Bullen.

'I agreed to your tapping my phone, Mr Foy. I did not agree to being shadowed. I should like your assurance that there will be no more of it.'

'It was for your own protection, sir.'

'I've long ceased worrying about protecting me. Have I your word?'

'Very well.'

'Good. Now I can tell you why I thought it necessary to dodge the policeman last night.'

He related the telephone conversations; and the renewed warning that the painting would be destroyed if he went to the police.

Foy reassured him. 'They're not going to destroy the only hold they have on you.'

'Many kidnappers have killed the person they kidnapped, while still pretending he was alive, in the hope of getting the ransom anyway.'

'A man is more difficult to keep concealed. If he is released, he may be able to give pointers to the kidnappers. None of that applies to a painting. I don't think you have to worry on that score. Anyhow, there's no need for them to know that you've told me what's happening. The vital thing is that you've established contact with people who undoubtedly hold the picture—the report from the lab on that scrap of canvas in the envelope establishes that. I'm returning it to you, by the way. You'd better hold it. Canvas and pigments are from a painting of the right date. It must be the Velazquez.'

'Agreed. So what do I do?'

After a pause for consideration, Foy said, 'I think it's probable that they're watching you. So we want to convince them that you're preparing to pay the ransom. These American dealers you were speaking of . . .'

Harrison had told him yesterday, Bullen replied, that a dealer named Joe Hymans, apparently one of the leaders in New York, representing at least three American oil millionaires, was still at Claridge's. He had been in touch with Harrison, making a private offer for the Velazquez, should it be recovered. 'I gather Hymans is offering a million and three quarters, and Harrison is sure he can be raised to a couple of million.'

'Then call on him today, please, Sir David. Go to Claridge's, make it as obvious as you can—ask for him loudly at the reception desk, perhaps go out somewhere to lunch with him, anything that can be easily noticed by an onlooker.'

'Do I tell him we're in touch and ask him for a quarter of a million in advance?'

'No, no. Not a word. Discuss with him the possibility

of a sale if and when the painting is recovered. But it will give the impression, if you're being watched, that you've gone to see him to raise the ransom. If you can, get him on any pretext to take you to his bank and introduce you to the manager. After that, sir, we'll have to be ready for whatever might follow.'

Foy pondered it throughout that morning. There was little enough to go on—but now it was evident that there was a criminal mind of high calibre involved, though it still had a hint of the gifted amateur.

There were at least three men taking part—the man who had impersonated Harrison, the man in the 'red-cheeked farmer' mask who had forced Harrison from his house at gunpoint, and the man who had driven the van in which he was taken to the West Country.

To the two first he had no lead whatsoever. The only fingerprints on the picture frame that were not those of the porters or the security men, were not in criminal records. Madge had had considerable hope of that mask, but he had found one that was on sale at fancy-goods shops all over the country, selling with party games and carnival accessories; and when he showed it to Harrison, he had confirmed it was the one. So that led nowhere. Harrison had not been able to identify the gun.

To the third man, the van driver, there was slightly more lead. Harrison, going through the photographs which Madge had shown him, had picked out three possibilities. Identification was uncertain because the lower half of the man's face had been hidden by a scarf. But the three Harrison picked were similar in appearance, which showed he had a fairly clear idea of the man's upper face.

Madge had turned up two of them so far. Each had an unquestionable alibi for the night. The third, Herbert George Shepherd, known as 'Boy' Shepherd and a car thief, had not as yet been traced. He was no longer in the Stepney district in which he usually lived; neither was the girl he lived with. He would be turned up sooner or later. Madge had high hopes of him. Foy was less convinced, but admitted it could be useful to ask him a question or two.

Nothing of the kind, however, could be counted on. He had to prepare for the actual attempt to collect the ransom. Not before Tuesday—that was the message Bullen had. Today was Friday. So they had four, probably five days at least in which to get ready.

There had to be a rendezvous at which a fairly large painting could be exchanged for two large suitcases ostensibly containing the money. The money itself was not much of a difficulty; forged notes were available that would pass at such a meeting. It must be secluded, and almost certainly in the open.

The vehicle in which the picture would be brought would certainly be stolen, and probably a small van. The men would probably be armed and ready to shoot their way out of trouble. Could he, therefore, risk Bullen as emissary? Foy did not like it, but it seemed inevitable. However, there was also to be an expert—he would be a police officer, of course, preferably armed. Foy hoped he could get permission for that. It might be possible to conceal one more officer in whatever vehicle Bullen used to get to the rendezvous, with radio communication that would enable police cars to follow at a distance and eventually draw a wide, narrowing cordon around the rendezvous.

Foy jotted one or two notes on his pad. It would have to be something like that.

The flat was small but well appointed. It had been converted from the top floor of one of the old houses—a sitting-room, bedroom, tiny kitchen squashed alongside the bathroom. When Frosso got there that first evening, a bunch of roses had been stuck in a vase on the living-room table; no note. She picked up the phone and heard the dialling tone, so it was connected. Presumably Hugh's little company took care of the phone bills too.

She wondered what girl friend of Hugh's had been living here before, and somewhat nervously went through the drawers and cupboards. But the linen was all new, unused. The place had been cleaned meticulously. There was a bottle of fresh milk in the fridge, tea in the canister, a jar of coffee beans beside the grinder and percolator on the kitchen shelf. She ground a handful of beans and switched on the percolator. While the coffee was making, she ran herself a warm bath. This part of the operation, at least, was comfortable enough.

As she was dressing, the phone rang. 'Everything all right?'

'Yes, fine, thank you.'

'I've got things more or less worked out. Meet at Sebastian's at eight o'clock tonight.'

Hugh was there when she arrived. Sebastian was sitting by the window, a gin in his hand. He gave her an irritable glance, but said nothing.

'I was telling Sebastian,' began Hugh, 'that the basic idea is to make the exchange, painting for money, in the midst of a lot of traffic, in daylight.'

'They're bound to spot us in Piccadilly Circus,' grunted Sebastian.

Hugh smiled. 'No doubt. That wasn't quite the place I was thinking of.'

'Aren't you going to let us in on the secret?'

'In time. The essential now is to be sure that Bullen has the money. I'm fairly sure that he can get it.'

He reported the watch he had kept on Bullen that day. He had gone to Claridge's soon after noon. Half an hour later he came out of the hotel with a thin, slight-looking, elderly American. Dell had checked on him afterwards; he was an art dealer named Hymans.

'Joe Hymans could certainly pay for the Velazquez,' put in Sebastian from the window seat. 'He's got the biggest string of oil millionaires in Texas. If the auction had gone through, it's quite likely Joe Hymans would have bought it. It's reckoned he can outbid even Wildenstein's for the really big stuff; though I doubt that.'

'But if Bullen is contemplating a private sale, to make sure he could get the ransom in advance . . .?'

'Then Hymans is probably the right man. He has clients who don't flinch at a gamble.'

Dell nodded, satisfied. For after Bullen and Hymans had lunched together at a restaurant in Jermyn Street, they had taken a taxi to the London bureau of one of the biggest of United States banks, and stayed there nearly an hour, seeing the manager. When they came out, Bullen shook Hymans by the hand, and they left in separate taxis.

'We ought to let Bullen know that we've watched him,' continued Dell reflectively. 'That means you phone him again this evening, Sebastian.'

'Go through all that business again?'

'Not necessary. Ring him at Sawdon House and tell him to go to the same place as last time, but to use the phone in the adjoining booth. You'll need the number—here it is.

'The police tap will know, of course, but I doubt if they could get a tap on the phone booth in time. Even if they do, it won't much matter. All you have to tell him is to follow up his meeting with Hymans, and make all necessary arrangements to collect the quarter-million in used notes in two large suitcases, at any time we instruct him to.

'Tell him, once he has made the arrangement, to put an advertisement in the Personal column of *The Times*, simply saying, "It's in the bag." Then wait until we give him further instructions. Okay?'

Sebastian nodded.

'This time,' said Hugh to Frosso, 'you'd better keep an eye on the phone booth at Tooting Bec. It's just possible that Bullen may have spotted me last time. I don't think he did, but we won't take even the slightest risk.

'What time shall we make your call, Sebastian? If you use public callboxes somewhere in Kensington, say, not far from here, you could ring Sawdon House at nine o'clock, and tell him to be at the Tooting Bec phone, waiting for a call, by 9.20. If you get there just before that time, Frosso, you'll need to keep an eye on him for only about five minutes. All we need is to be sure he's alone, and not being followed. There's a dress shop not far away. You can be staring at the dresses in the window.'

So she took a taxi to Balham and strolled leisurely along the High Road towards the dress-shop window. A Negro with narrow hips and long arms tried to pick her up, but she spat a couple of suitable words at him and he wandered away, disconcerted.

Almost to the minute Bullen emerged from the Underground and entered the callbox, thumbing through the directory as though looking for a number. Frosso waited. It seemed a long wait, but her watch told her it was only just over one minute. Then he picked up the phone and began speaking. From the window of the dress shop she looked cautiously round. Nobody, so far as she could see, had followed Bullen from the Underground and loitered near him. There was a thin soaking of rain and the pavements were almost empty. When Bullen emerged, and re-entered the station, Frosso followed him. She could see nobody else doing so.

She took a ticket to Sloane Square. Down below, on

the platform, she came face to face with him. But he did not even look at her. His gaze was fixed on thoughts inside his head She watched him into the train before she entered the next compartment. He got off at Clapham North.

Then she relaxed, realizing how strung she had been. The relaxing was enjoyable; but the tension had been superb.

Bullen on the phone to Foy: 'Yes, the same man rang me last night. I couldn't be mistaken about that voice. It's as fake as ever.

'You were quite right. Somebody must have been watching when I went to see Hymans yesterday. The man on the phone knew about it, and knew we had been to Hymans's bank. He asked if I had been broaching the subject of raising part of the sale price in advance, on Hymans's say-so to his banker. I said I had. I said that Hymans had telephoned one of his clients in America to ask if he would gamble a quarter of a million pounds, on the prospect of getting the Velazquez for two million if we could recover it. I said that Hymans's client had agreed, snap, like that, on the spot.

'It was all complete fabrication. All I really told Hymans was that the police had good hopes of recovering the painting. If they did, I proposed to sell it privately for around £2 million. He said he would be interested. I then suggested—rather lamely, I thought, but he agreed—that we go to see his banker, to make sure the money would be forthcoming.

'It was a ridiculous interview with Hymans's banker. Both of them guessed I was after something quite different from what I was saying, and were extremely curious. However, after a completely inconsequential half-hour, out we came, Hymans and I, and I shook hands ostentatiously with him. Whoever was watching saw that too. The man on the phone mentioned it, as a pointer to Hymans's acceptance of the gamble. No, I didn't spot anyone following me. I don't know where he was, or how it was done.

'But now I have the first part of my instructions. I am to arrange with the banker to be able to collect the quarter-million in old £5 and £1 notes whenever I want to. When that is fixed, I am to insert a given advertisement in *The Times* Personal column. Then I await further orders.

'Of course, I shan't make any such arrangement with the banker. But you're going to have to take him to some extent into your confidence, Foy. At some time he has to allow me to call at his bank and collect two large suitcases, supposedly filled with notes. I leave that to you to arrange. And you must get the suitcases round to the bank, filled with whatever seems to you suitable.

'Do you think there's any chance we shall pull this off? Get the picture back? I know your chief aim is to catch the criminals. Mine isn't. I don't give a hoot whether they are caught or not, provided I get that picture back. However, I dare say both our aims will fit together when the time comes.

'So what now? I take it I just put the ad in *The Times* on, say, Tuesday of next week, to make it feasible that I contacted the banker on Monday. Then sit back until I get the next phone call.

'My car? It's an elderly Bentley. A policeman in the boot? Well, I suppose you could get a small man in. There's not a lot of room, and he'd be damned uncomfortable. It's in a lock-up garage at the end of this street. By all means send a man to inspect it. Ring Rose Pearson—she has the key to the garage. Electronic equipment? Oh, put in anything you like. You don't have to thank me, Foy. I want that painting back, desperately.'

When she sleepily opened her eyes, Frosso saw that it was already morning. Hugh was still asleep on the pillow beside her. Asleep, he showed his age more clearly than when he was up and groomed. The stubble of beard on his jaw was mostly grey. The skin of his face had loosened a little. There was a slight stain of saliva at the corner of his mouth.

She had known, of course, that they would go to bed together; had been somewhat irritated that he had waited those four days since putting her in the flat, without any indication. But then had come the phone call abruptly inviting her to dinner.

'Why don't we eat here?' she had suggested. 'There might be a risk if somebody who knows me, and knows I'm at Crosby's, happens to see us in a restaurant.' The invitation, of course, was blatant.

'Thanks.'

'I'll cook the meal. You bring whatever wine you want to drink. About eight o'clock.'

Throughout the evening he had said not one word about the picture or the enterprise. She was grateful for that. She had led him to tell her something about himself. He gave only fragments. As a youngster he had just managed to get into the last few weeks of the Allied advance through Germany in 1945, and had then taken part in the occupation of Berlin; stories of the suffering, the violence, the black market festering amid the ruins. He had seen fighting in Korea—and much else that went on there, he cynically hinted. There were disconnected tales of adventures, many of them scurrilous, in Australia, in Burma, in Ecuador and Brazil; tales of gun-running, smuggling, gambling, of an uncounted stream of rogues, and women. The grimmest stories were of the mercenary campaigns in the Congo, where he served in Tshombe's Fifth Commando, and then later in Angola; not much about Nigeria. And at last, almost without preliminaries, he had taken her to bed.

Frosso gazed with curiosity at his sleeping head on the pillow. She had anticipated that he would be efficient and not in the least gentle. She had not expected him to be so completely without emotion, so absolutely physical. Even after sleep, her body was aching, and she could feel the bruising of her thighs.

She eased herself from the bed and went to the bathroom to take a shower, fix her face and her hair, put on a wrap. Then she went through to the kitchen to percolate coffee and open a can of orange juice.

When she came out with the tray he was no longer in the bed. She could hear the shower in the bathroom, then the hum of an electric razor. He emerged trim, with a bath towel tied round his waist.

'Where did you get the razor?'

'I keep one here. It was in the back of the medicine cupboard.' He saw the momentary frown. 'Oh, come on. You knew perfectly well that I had another girl here before. We're not starting a lifelong liaison, after all.'

'Just what are we starting?'

'Need it be the start of anything?' he asked, taking the cup of coffee with a nod and reaching for his glass of orange juice. 'A pleasant night together, just that. I hope you found it pleasant.'

'There were moments—none of them particularly sentimental.'

Hugh smiled. 'You like it sentimental? Is that what Sebastian gave you? I wondered.'

She said nothing, but filled her own cup and sat sipping the coffee.

'We ought to have a quiet talk about Sebastian,' he said. 'I have a plan worked out for the ransom which

I'm pretty sure will do. But it has one weakness—Sebastian. What's he going to be like in a crisis? He might crack. That could land us all in it. We ought to shake Sebastian out of it, you and I. We could handle it far more efficiently, just the two of us. And wouldn't the money seem better divided into two instead of three?'

'Sebastian has the painting.'

Hugh sighed. 'Yes, that's right. And, of course, he knows too much. It's not practical. Pity!'

The phone rang. Frosso looked startled, glancing at her watch. But Hugh motioned to her to answer it.

'Frosso? Have you seen *The Times* this morning? The ad's in. I've tried to get Hugh at the number he gave us, but there's no reply.'

'He'll see the ad. I expect he'll ring both of us later. Yes, of course I'm all right.'

She hung up. Turning to Hugh, she said, 'Sebastian. He says the ad's in *The Times*.'

Hugh stood up to reach for his clothes. 'Right. Meet me at Sebastian's, usual time tonight. We're in business.'

CHAPTER XI

Buzzing for Madge, Foy instructed, 'Bring in the whole scheme. It looks as though it's tomorrow.'

Madge came in with the folder of orders, details of the radio links and codes, the coded road maps. 'Tomorrow, sir?'

'I've just had Bullen on the phone. Ten minutes ago he got a note—one of the kids staying at Sawdon House brought it up to his office. The boy said a lady gave it to him in the street, just round the corner, and promised he'd get 10p if he delivered it to Bullen. So there's a woman in it, Madge, as well as the three men. The boy could describe her only vaguely—doesn't seem to have been a very bright boy. Pretty, with dark hair—that's all. Still, Bullen gave him his 10p.'

'What sort of note, sir?'

'Typed in capitals on typing paper you can buy anywhere, in the cheapest manila envelope.'

'Typed? Then it could be identified.'

'Maybe, if we ever get anywhere near the typewriter. What the note said is: "The signal you'll get tomorrow is three rings on the telephone and no caller. If you are able to produce the money, put a carnation in your buttonhole and drive in your own car to wherever you are to collect it. You may pick up your art expert, but nobody else in the car. Don't communicate with anyone. Drive to Barnes Common. If any suspicious sign seen, or any car tailing you, the picture will be destroyed. At Barnes station buy a ticket to Kew Gardens."'

'Barnes station, sir? What do we do? Cover it?'

Foy shook his head slowly. 'We mustn't go anywhere near it. My guess is that they're trying to find out whether Bullen is telling us anything or not. If anyone like a policeman turns up at Barnes station today or tomorrow, they'll vanish, and we'll have lost the trail.'

'The carnation in the buttonhole sounds as though Bullen is to meet somebody who hasn't seen him, sir.'

'Yes. Our only course is to play along with whatever they tell Bullen to do, until the actual moment when they're to hand over the painting and take the money. You've got the list of patrols approved? Get them on stand-by from 06.00 hours tomorrow. I'll hold a briefing at 08.00.'

When he was alone, Foy spread out the road maps and tried to guess. Barnes was just the gambit. The rendezvous would have to be distant from London and much more remote from traffic, so that no police car could approach without being seen.

Foy put his chin in his fist. What was his answer to the gambit? What, first of all, was the opening position?

The two suitcases were already in the American bank. The banker had been most co-operative, not asking questions, although he must have guessed, after Bullen's visit with Hymans, roughly what it was about. The cases were packed with £250,000 in used £5 and £1 notes, all forgeries. They had been used once before, in a notorious kidnap case some years earlier. In that case the bait had not been taken, the notes had not been collected. Foy hoped that wasn't an omen.

If they were collected, he reckoned they'd pass any hasty inspection—unless the man inspecting them was a currency expert, and he'd then at once detect the forgeries. But even if that happened, Foy calculated that he ought to have the police cordon drawn sufficiently close to make the catch.

Madge had objected that they'd still have the Velazquez to use as hostage, but Foy had merely shrugged. That hostage wouldn't do for him. If it were lost there would be a public howl. Well, let them howl. He did not feel too great a concern about the painting. He was after the men.

Unless the police were armed, the villains might shoot their way through the cordon—a more valid objection. Foy had put it up to the Commissioner, who had taken it up in the greatest secrecy with the Home Secretary; and arms had been refused. There had been no serious violence in the thing so far. The Home Secretary did not feel he could authorize arming the police on the grounds of the pistol that had held up Harrison. So it had to be unarmed.

In one way, that was a relief to Foy. He could not for a moment forget that he was exposing two civilians to whatever happened—Sir David Bullen and Charles

Harrison. Bullen had refused to take a policeman posing as an art expert. He insisted on a real expert. Harrison had joyfully agreed to go with him.

There would necessarily be, as the cordon closed in, quite a time during which no policeman would be near enough to help those two men, except the communications man in the boot. Foy tried to put from his mind the possibility that they might be seized as human hostages.

He stared at the maps. If only he had an inkling which way they'd be going. There were open spaces without much traffic in almost any direction around London. All he could do was form his screen of police cars in an outer circle, moving with Bullen's car as its centre. For the route he would have to rely on radioed news from the man hidden in the boot of the Bentley—radioed to Foy, in his control car a mile or so behind.

Foy sighed. Even on paper the loopholes were glaring. What would matter, when the time came, was how quickly and accurately he could appreciate the situation, how effectively bring his cordon in. He wished he could feel happier about it.

The first thing that Hugh Dell did on that Wednesday morning was to telephone Freddie, the man who had put him in touch with Sebastian in the first place, and then with 'Boy' Shepherd for the van business. Freddie confirmed that the three vehicles he wanted had been 'collected' and prepared. Yes, he had used Boy again, but there was no risk there.

The number plates had all been changed. The light van had been re-sprayed blue. The Mini was now dark green. There were so many grey Jaguars about that it had not been thought necessary to change the colour of that one.

All three vehicles were in good working order, everything ready for driving off. There would be no need to put in at a petrol station in less than a couple of hundred miles. The vehicles were all in the garage in the mews in Earls Court of which he already had the key. Freddie took it that, when the cars were finished with, they would all be abandoned in different places.

'Right,' agreed Dell. 'I'll go to the mews to look them over this afternoon, and leave your money in a briefcase on the back seat of the Jag. Can you collect it this evening? I'll send back the key to the garage by post tomorrow.'

Next he rang Sebastian. 'Will you be in the shop for the next hour? I'm coming round.'

He did not much like the look of Sebastian when he got there. He was restless with nerves. His cheerfulness was forced. The man was plain frightened—and, by the look in his eyes, had been drugging to quieten his fears. Dell said nothing. A resentful man might be an even worse risk than a man sedated with drugs.

A woman came into the shop, enquiring the price of a pair of cut-glass decanters in the window. Dell busied himself examining an untidy heap of tattered prints until, after long discussion, she had bought a china shepherdess and departed.

'All the transport is arranged,' he then told Sebastian, 'except your own van. Have you had it serviced? It looks a bit ropey. I suppose it's good for anything up to a hundred miles?'

'It's looked like that for seven years. Goes like a two-year-old.'

'Let's hope so.'

'I take it the painting goes out in it?'

'No,' said Dell abruptly. 'But if the plan doesn't come off, the painting will come back in it. When we meet tonight I'll give you the whole plan in detail. But what we have to have is the painting, here in this building, either in the room above, or preferably down here in the shop.'

Sebastian looked uneasy. 'Do we have to take the painting out at all? Seems to me one hell of a risk. If there were the slightest accident, anyone who happened to see it would know at once it was the Velazquez. Why can't we just collect the money, and fool him?'

'Bullen won't part until his expert confirms the painting.'

'Once we've got them out somewhere with the money in used notes—well, it doesn't sound too difficult to get hold of it for a determined man like you.'

'There'd be no point. Once we have the money, the painting has no value for us. Bullen certainly won't cough up a second ransom—probably couldn't raise one, anyhow. And we couldn't sell it. It would be a perpetual danger to whoever held it—to you, if you held it. There would always be the risk that, some day, it would be seen. Once we have the money, the only thing is to get rid of the picture—and what better way of doing that than handing it over to Bullen? Where is it?'

Sebastian muttered sullenly that he didn't need to know until tonight.

'I need to know now.'

Sebastian hesitated, tried to stare into Dell's eyes, then dropped his own gaze.

From a stack of old pictures piled against the back wall of the shop he lugged out a large oil of Italian scenery—castles on hilltops, half-naked nymphs in the valley pools—in a battered gilt frame. 'It's fastened in the frame behind this canvas.'

Dell smiled slowly. That wasn't bad. He reckoned it could stay there throughout most of the journey. 'Is it easily detached?' he asked. 'You don't need tools?'

'No. It's held in by four wooden clips. All you do is turn them, and it pulls out at the back. Do you want to see it?'

'Take your word for it, Sebastian. Because one thing is certain—if we don't all three trust each other implicitly for the next twenty-four hours, we might as well start deciding what further-education course to take in gaol.'

He almost laughed at the man's wry expression.

'See you tonight,' he said, leaving the shop.

By then he had checked the vehicles in the mews garage, gone for a brisk walk to exercise his muscles and ease his nerves, taken a warm bath at his flat, forced himself to eat a very light meal, limited his drink to one rather generous scotch, and tried to turn his thoughts away from the morrow. None of this worried him. It used to, years before. But he knew now that he was always like this before a battle, or a crime—or a new woman. When the time came, he was all right again.

He deliberately got to Sebastian's late, so that they were both waiting for him.

Clearing the junk from a table, he spread out a sketch map of the café and the adjoining car and lorry parks. The important factors, he emphasized, were the placing of the transport and the timing. He did not think Bullen had gone to the police, but had planned on the assumption that he might have done so, and therefore deception would be necessary, and concentration on the getaway.

'You, Frosso, will be driving the Mini. You must get there slightly before either Sebastian or myself, because you have to give a message to the woman at the cash desk. You should be there not long after 13.30 hours, and not later than 13.45. This end, as you see—' pointing to the map—'is the park for private cars. It'll be fairly full, but the turnover is rapid. Park in a position from which the Mini can get easily to the exit, here, without obstruction. That means it has really got to be either in the front row, or the back row. Make it the back row if you can.

'Leave the Mini unlocked, with the ignition key hidden under a book on the shelf. Then go to the self-service café and bribe the woman at the cash desk to give this note to Bullen when he arrives. If she won't, you'll have to wait around out of sight, and then tip a waitress to take him the note. In either case, it's vital to see that the note reaches Bullen. If anything goes wrong with that, return to the Mini and put a newspaper on the seat. That will be the signal to cancel the whole operation. The blue van will be there by then, and we'll all come away in it. Is that clear so far?'

Frosso nodded, eyes intent.

'By the way, you've told your office that you're sick and won't be in tomorrow?'

'Yes. And Charles said it wouldn't matter, since he would be away himself.' She laughed. 'He cooked up the most elaborate story about a business appointment in Brighton.'

'Good,' said Dell. 'Now, once Bullen has that note, keep out of the way. But you must be able to watch the front entrance to the café. Both the men will go out to the car park. Some time later—at least a quarter of an hour, probably longer—both of them will come back, and re-enter the café. Directly you see that, come along the back of the car park until you find the Jaguar. It'll be somewhere near where you left the Mini. Sebastian and I will be in the front seats. Get into the back, without talking, and we're off. Anything you want to question?'

Frosso shook her head.

'Sebastian, you will be driving the blue van, with the Velazquez in the back, still hidden behind the other one in that gilt frame. If anyone should look into the back of the van, all he'll see is an old Italian oil painting, so there's no risk to you. You're a picture dealer. You often carry that sort of junk around.

'By 13.30 hours you must be in this country lane, where your own old van will be parked—you and I will take it out there tonight, directly it's dark, and leave it there. It's a lonely spot. It won't be noticed.

'When you get there tomorrow, pull up the blue van behind it, detach the *Venus* in the blue van, and put the old Italian picture and the frame into your own van and lock it.

'Follow the lane to this corner, turn left along this road, and you should get to the café in about ten minutes, in the blue van, with the Velazquez in the back. The truck park, as you see from the sketch map, is at this other end. Park the van there, right away from the road exit. Leave it locked, and come round the back of the café to the car park. You'll find the Jaguar there, with me in it. We'll sit there, pretending to have a picnic —as though we've been inside to get cans of beer and carried them out to eat snacks in the car.

'From then on, leave everything to me. If all goes well, the ransom will be put in the Mini. When I say so, we lift the suitcases from the Mini into the Jaguar, Frosso joins us, and we leave. We drive the Jaguar to your old van parked in the lane and abandon it there. We all come home in your old van—with a quarter of a million quid.

'But, if anything goes wrong, we abandon both the Mini and the Jaguar in the café car park—and the money—and make for the blue van. All three of us—is that clear? Good. Nobody must be left stranded without a vehicle to come away in. It takes some explaining if you're on a motorway without a vehicle. So we leave in the blue van, drive it to Sebastian's old van in the lane, make the transfer there, and all come home in Sebastian's van, without the money—but with the Velazquez.

'I'm not going to ask if you can see any snags. I can see a dozen myself. But that's the plan, and it stands. If a crisis arises, I'll cope—and rely on both of you to do whatever I tell you, fast, and without question. In this sort of operation, that's the only way.'

'Sure,' agreed Sebastian—but grudgingly—more reluctantly than Dell could have wished. Dell's doubts of the man strengthened. But from now on, unless they called the whole thing off, they were committed. That was the plan. He would not change it.

CHAPTER XII

The phone in Bullen's office rang three times at 10.45 hours on the Thursday morning. He lifted the receiver. As the callbox pips started, the caller hung up and the dialling tone purred.

'That's it,' announced Bullen cheerfully. He had not felt so exhilarated for years.

'Take care, won't you?' from Rose, putting the carnation, as instructed, in his buttonhole.

'As much care as usual, I promise you that.'

He backed his Bentley out of the garage. The policeman, he knew, would by now have cramped himself into the boot, lying on a rubber mattress, surrounded by electronics, in touch with Foy in his control car waiting in Richmond Park. Foy would have been told by the Yard man listening on Bullen's telephone line that the starting signal had been given.

As Bullen turned north across Battersea Bridge, heading through thick traffic for Harrison's house, the voice of the policeman in the boot whispered electronically,

'Everything's in position, Sir David. I'm in touch with Mr Foy. The whole operation's ready to move.'

'Hope you're not too uncomfortable,' said Bullen into the small microphone pinned to the steering column.

'I rehearsed it in another Bentley. Stayed inside for six hours. Didn't feel too good when I came out. But I'll manage, sir.'

Charles Harrison had dressed for the occasion in a thick black high-necked sweater and heavy cord trousers. Bullen asked about the bulge in his pocket, and he produced a short length of lead pipe. It wouldn't do, he declared, to be defenceless if it came to a scrap. Bullen smiled and advised him to put it on the floor. 'It isn't going to come to a scrap.'

The manager was waiting for Bullen's arrival at the American bank. He gestured to the bank guard, who took two large suitcases out to the Bentley. Bullen nodded his thanks and drove off, turning west through Kensington to re-cross the Thames at Hammersmith Bridge. The traffic widened out along Castelnau and across Barnes Common. Bullen pulled up by the station, touched the carnation for luck, and went down the steps to the booking hall. 'Single to Kew Gardens, please.'

'Ah,' said the booking clerk, 'you're the chap in the treasure hunt, then?'

'Treasure hunt?'

'Young lady in here this morning, said the chaps from your motoring club in the treasure hunt would be wearing carnations, and would ask for tickets to Kew Gardens . . .'

Catching on, Bullen said, 'You're the next clue, then? By damn, that's clever of them. Yes, I'm in the treasure hunt. It's great fun. What's the clue?'

The clerk handed him a manila envelope. 'Looks like you've won, then. The young lady says this is the last clue. Give it to the first chap who gets here, and tell all the others who turn up to go back to the clubhouse.'

Bullen beamed. 'Oh, that's great news. Thanks.'

Back in the car, he ripped the envelope. Inside was a small sheet of paper, typed in capitals. He read the message out slowly, so that the man in the boot could get it. 'A413 and A43 to Northampton. Buy a drink in the saloon bar at the Chequers. Identify yourself to the manager with your driving licence.'

'Okay sir,' came the whisper from the boot. 'I've passed it to control.'

Reaching for his AA road book, Bullen worked out the route. 'Tell Mr Foy I'm turning back over Hammersmith Bridge, then Hammersmith Road, Holland Road, and on to the A40. I'll turn off at Gerrards Cross on to the A413. Then it's direct. Tell him not to try to cut in on that pub at Northampton.'

Looking at his watch, he saw it was close on 11.30. They ought to get to Northampton, he told Harrison, at about half past one, or perhaps a quarter to two, depending on the traffic across London.

The voice from the boot: 'Super says he won't go anywhere near the pub, or anywhere else that's named, until it's clear, from me, that the handover's about to take place. The cordon is moving round us and will circle Northampton, but won't go into the town.'

'What's the idea of all this dodging about?' asked Charles.

'I imagine it's to give them a chance to watch us, whoever they are, and make sure there are only two of us in the car, and no police escort tailing us.'

He and Harrison did not speak much as he drove across London. Traffic was heavy and Bullen made bad time. Once he was on the A40 he let the car out a bit, but the A413 was not a fast road, and the A43 not much better. It was after 13.30 when they reached Northampton, found the Chequers and went into the saloon bar.

Bullen ordered two pints of bitter and asked for the manager. A dapper man came out from behind.

'I'm Sir David Bullen.' He got out his driving licence.

'Oh, Sir David, I'm so sorry to hear of your little boy's illness.'

'Kind of you,' murmured Bullen.

'Your sister told me about it when she came in this morning, only an hour ago. She gave me this letter for you. It's the letter from the Harley Street consultant that the doctor will want in Carlisle. I'm so glad I've been able to help get the letter to you. She said it was the only way she could think of.'

'It's a great relief,' Bullen told him, putting the letter in his pocket. 'Come on, Charles, we must be off.' They drained their pints and left, the manager's solicitude following them out into the road.

Bullen drove round the corner before stopping to open the envelope. Again he read out the typed message: 'Get on the M1 at Junction 15 and turn north. At the northbound service station on the motorway, halfway between Junctions 15 and 16, park your car and both of you go into the self-service café. Pick up snacks at the counter. When you pay, ask the woman at the cash desk whether the manager's name is Wilberforce.'

From the boot: 'Transmitted, sir.'

As they turned from the motorway, Charles complained, 'This is getting ridiculous.'

Bullen's face was set grimly. 'If you ask me, we're nearly there.' To the boot he said, 'Put it to Mr Foy. Wouldn't the huge, busy car park of a service station on the motorway be a good choice for the swap?'

Minutes later, from the boot: 'Mr Foy agrees with you, sir. He's closing the cordon in gradually now.'

Not for a moment was the scene empty. From a window in the women's lavatory of the service station Frosso was gazing at the ceaseless streams of traffic flowing in the distance south/north and, beyond, north/south along the M1, the spinal motorway of the country; huge trucks and lorries in the nearside lanes, vans and cars in the centre, and the speeding fresco of the fast lanes; and always the traffic roar, strengthening or weakening from minute to minute, but never stopping.

She could see the main entrance to the parking sites through which northbound lorries, trucks, vans and cars were turning in from the motorway almost without pause; and the distant exit road through which she could just see an even denser stream rumbling outwards.

The parking sites were crammed. But continually some vehicles were leaving, the gaps quickly filled by new arrivals jostling for a space. She had had to wait several minutes, but had then been able to slip the Mini into the back row, close to the end nearest the exit lane. On her way to the café she had turned to glance back and had seen Hugh nosing the grey Jaguar towards the back row of the park.

Inside it was even noisier—the clatter of crockery and cutlery, scraping of feet on the vinyl floor, the chattering roar of people talking. There was such a queue at the self-service counter that Frosso squirmed along to the cash desk at the end and managed to hold the cashier's attention long enough to slip her £1. Then she had been co-operative. 'Okay, love. I understand. That'll be the fifth motoring treasure hunt we've had through here already this summer. I give this envelope, eh? to the first fellow who comes along with a carnation in his buttonhole and uses the password—asks if the manager's name is Wilberforce.' She giggled. 'Matter of fact, love, his name's Blogg.'

Frosso had laughed dutifully and left her to it. As a precaution she had a duplicate of the message in her handbag, so that she could make a second attempt, if need be, to get it to Bullen.

If, that was, he came at all. She did not know whether the treasure-hunt clue she had left at Barnes station, or the story she had cooked up in the Northampton pub about Bullen's little boy being ill, had worked properly.

As she had made her way to the women's lavatory and found a cubicle from which she could look on to the car park, Frosso had wondered whether Sebastion had arrived while she was talking to the cashier. She had a horrible fear that he would be late, or even that he might have lost his nerve and turned back, cooking up some story to Hugh of a breakdown.

She wondered what Hugh would do to him if that happened.

Then she told herself she had better stop wondering about that or anything else. The thing had started. Since Hugh, who had been checking near Barnes, had already arrived, Bullen must at least have picked up the message at the station there. And if anything went wrong from now on, they had their escape drill planned.

Suddenly she caught a glimpse of a small blue van in the huddle of vehicles coming on to the park. For a moment a large lorry blotted the van from her view. But as the lorry moved ahead she could see the van clearly, and Sebastian at the wheel; too far off to see how he was looking, how well he was taking it, but at least he was there.

So the thing was on.

She felt the sudden quiver of her nerves which had been lacking throughout the morning; until then she had seemed to herself almost listless; perhaps, she had thought, the excitement ended once the actual operation began. But no. The exquisite shudder seized her again, and the operation had in fact begun—provided, of course, that Bullen himself arrived.

She looked round the park, then drew in her breath,

startled. Charles was walking from the cars towards the café entrance. Then beside him she saw Bullen. She had missed the arrival of the Bentley in that kaleidoscope of vehicles. How ridiculous Charles looked in that black sweater and those thick trousers—as though he had got himself up for the hero's part in a television toughie. She smiled a little, regretting that she would never be able to tell him what an idiot he had looked.

Waiting until the two men had had time to get inside the self-service wing, she hurried to a small landing on the staircase. There she could seem to be looking at tawdry souvenirs and gifts displayed in a brightly-lit showcase, but could in fact, through a window-light beside it, look down into the café. Bullen and Charles had already taken up a position at the end of the long queue to the counter.

Three men were sitting in three different vehicles, tensely waiting for the thing to develop.

One was Chief Detective Superintendent Foy. He had halted his control car in a lay-by near the approach road to motorway Junction 15. With the map open before him, he was trying to decide how close in to bring the cordon.

He no longer had much guidance from Bullen's car. The man there had reported that Bullen and Harrison had gone towards the café. From now on he could report only what he might be able to see through the periscope peepholes which had been arranged to give him a limited forward view; or anything that Bullen might tell him if he returned to the car.

Foy was now certain that the exchange was planned for in or near the service station. He ordered one car of four plain-clothes men to stand by, ready to proceed to the service-station car park. He ordered two more cars, once the operation started, to get as fast as they could on to the northbound carriageway of the motorway itself. They would then pull up on to the emergency verge, one south of the service station, the other north of it, and open car bonnets, probing the engines as though in a breakdown.

That was his striking force.

The remainder—nine cars carrying thirty-six men—he ordered to close in on the motorway junctions, but not to move on to the road itself.

Then he turned to Sergeant Madge, in his seat by the driver. 'For God's sake, Madge, let's have a drink.'

'Coming up, sir,' said Madge, reaching for the basket at his feet, passing round sandwiches and opening the cans of beer.

The second man waiting for the thing to develop was Hugh Dell in the grey Jaguar parked at the service station. He had managed to park only three cars distant from the Mini, so he knew that Frosso was in position. Since parking the car, he had made one sortie to the lorry park at the other end of the site. He had watched the arrival of a black furniture van, seen its elderly driver and his mate move leisurely towards the café, decided that one would do, and chalked a brief message on its back. Then he had returned to the Jaguar, prepared a note, put it into an envelope with a key, and had nothing more to do except wait for Sebastian to arrive.

For a few moments he wondered if Sebastian had chickened; by the glimpse Hugh caught of the whiteness of the man's face when at last the blue van arrived, it had been a near thing. But no matter. He was there. The Velazquez was there. Not long afterwards he saw Bullen's Bentley arrive.

If Frosso had done her part inside the café—and Hugh was sure she had—the operation was working.

The third waiting man was Sebastian Hurley, in the blue van. He should not have been waiting. His orders from Dell were to leave the van at once and make his way round the back of the café, to find him in the Jaguar.

But the hell with Dell. He was too bloody free with his orders. Sebastian needed a few minutes to calm himself. Driving north and transferring the Italian oil in its frame from the blue van into his own old van parked in that lane had been nervy enough. Suppose he were stopped. Even before the *Venus* was uncovered, he felt sure he would have given himself away. And once the Velazquez was lying exposed in the blue van, the risk seemed so formidable that he contemplated abandoning the whole thing—van, painting and all—and running for it. But one-third of a quarter of a million quid was a lot of money.

It ought to have been nearly one-half, Sebastian told himself bitterly. But at least, when he and Frosso went off together, they would have two-thirds between them. He had plans for their future—South American plans. So his nerve had to hold out.

The worst part was coming—the period of tension, of possible disaster. All the time he was sitting in the blue van in that park, he had been fighting temptation. Now he surrendered. He felt for the syringe in his pocket, rolled back his cuff and gave himself a shot. After a few minutes, when he had quietened, he left the van and circled round the back of the service station, to look for Dell in the Jaguar.

As he and Harrison worked their way in the queue along the self-service counter, Bullen glanced round as casually as he could. But he could see nothing, in all that scramble and roar of people, that seemed in the least suspicious. No doubt they were being watched but it was impossible to spot the watcher.

Harrison was grumbling at the food. 'You can't

expect me to eat any of that, my dear Bullen.'

'Try a ham roll, or one of these delicious pork pies.' He grinned at the look on Harrison's face as he lifted one on to his plate. 'We'll get ourselves coffee, then you take the food and find a table. Leave the paying to me.'

When he reached the cash desk, he asked the woman, 'Is the manager's name Wilberforce?'

'Ah, you're the first,' she said, reaching beneath the counter for the envelope.

Guessing it was the treasure hunt again, Bullen smiled, pointed to his carnation and asked, 'Is that the clue?'

'That's what the girl said, love. Except she said the winner'd give me a quid for the envelope.'

'Of course.'

Pocketing the pound, the cashier reflected that there was always the possibility of a little extra profit.

Sitting beside Harrison, Bullen carefully took a sip of coffee, then a munch of ham roll, before looking at the envelope. On the back was printed, in ballpoint, 'Mini RDY 565. Parked in the back row.'

He tore open the envelope, read the instruction typed on the sheet inside, then passed it over to Harrison. 'Get one suitcase from your car. Carry it yourself, without the other man. Put it in the car identified on the back of this envelope. Return at once to your own car, stay inside it for five minutes, then return to the ransom car. If everything's in order, you'll be directed to the picture.'

'We're off, then,' said Harrison, excited.

'Finish your pork pie first,' replied Bullen, munching his. 'Operational meal before the fun starts.'

When he had drunk his coffee they went back to the Bentley.

Bullen lifted out one of the suitcases, whispering towards the steering column, 'I'm leaving the note here. Mr Harrison will read it to you while I'm away. Get in the back, Charles, and lock yourself in.' To the boot he added, 'There's just a chance that they'll try for this second bag while they think there's only one man in the car.'

'Don't worry, sir. I'm watching.'

Bullen found the Mini after walking nearly the whole length of the back row. The interior was bare. Bullen put the suitcase on the seat, shut the door and walked away without looking back.

In the Bentley again, he said, 'Tell Mr Foy it's a dark green Mini parked nearly at the road end of the back row.' He looked at his watch, smiled at Harrison, remarked, 'Now we have five minutes for contemplation —and digestion. Not sure I was right, after all, about those pork pies.'

It was a crowded five minutes for Dell.

Sitting in the Jaguar with the picnic laid out beside him, pretending to read a newspaper, he had watched Bullen putting the suitcase in the Mini, then going back towards his own car. Dell gave him a minute to get clear, then eased himself from the Jaguar, walked carelessly over to the Mini, pulled out a wallet of car keys with which he feigned to open the already unlocked door, and lifted the lid of the suitcase.

He slid his fingers under the top layers to make sure the notes went right down to the base. Pulling a couple from their paper band, he turned them over, studied them as well as he could under cover of the suitcase lid. They seemed all right. He shut the suitcase, put the envelope containing a note and the key on top of its lid, pretended to relock the Mini door, and went by a roundabout route back to the Jaguar.

As he slid in, he looked at his watch. Bullen should be back in just one minute.

'The money there?' whispered Sebastian, tense.

'Yes.'

'Why didn't you bring it here? We'd have had half of it, whatever happens.'

'If anything happens, I don't want any part of the money in the same car as myself. If anything happens, we take back the picture, and that's all. Now shut up.'

In his control car parked in the lay-by, Francis Foy was irritable too. He had the message from the Bentley that Bullen was putting half the ransom in the Mini, registration RDY 565. A few minutes later he had the further message from the Bentley that Bullen had returned, had five minutes to wait, and had identified the Mini, dark green, parked near the road end of the back row.

Foy swore softly at himself, afraid that over-cautiously he had delayed too long. Now he jerked out an order to the three cars of the striking force to get into position. But they could scarely get there in less than five or six minutes.

'There's a change in the plan. The car going into the park is to pinpoint a dark green Mini, RDY 565, and keep it under observation and report any activity around it. Don't make any move until you get an order from me, or unless anybody goes to that Mini. If anyone does, tell me, and one man is to tail him. If there's an attempt to drive the Mini out, grab it. The picture can't be in the Mini. If it's there at all, it'll be in a van in the lorry park. But that can wait. We want the men. If we get the men, we can get the picture later. If any of you slips, so that we get the picture and lose the men, I personally will see that he goes back on the beat for the rest of his service. So watch it.' He switched to the outer ring of cars. 'Start moving, every car. Close on the service station. Get set for action directly you get the order.'

CHAPTER XIII

Bullen waited exactly five minutes. Then he got out of the Bentley, murmuring to Harrison, 'Hang on here. I won't be long.'

He walked sharply towards the Mini. Opening the door, he saw the envelope on top of the suitcase.

He ripped it open. A small key dropped into his palm. Fiddling with his fingers, he drew out a note: 'The key unlocks the rear door of a black furniture van in the second row of the lorry park, registration ARU 125B. When your expert is satisfied that the Velazquez is genuine, lock the van, fetch the remainder of the ransom from your car, put it into the Mini, return to the café and remain there for fifteen minutes. Then you may call the police. Don't touch the painting until you get an Army bomb expert to it. It's booby-trapped. If you attempt any double-cross, the booby-trap will be exploded by remote control.'

Bullen walked back to his own car. He was beginning to disbelieve all this. The booby-trap nonsense, though possible, was unlikely—too complicated, too elaborate. His guess was that he and Harrison would be sent off to the lorry park to look for a non-existent black furniture van, and the thieves would make off with the half-ransom in the Mini. It was a consolation that all the notes in the suitcase were forgeries. But that would not return his picture.

When he got back to the Bentley, he said for the benefit of the man in the boot, 'We've got our instructions, Charles. This key is said to unlock the rear door of a black furniture van, registration ARU 125B, in the second row of the lorry park. The Velazquez is said to be inside, with a booby-trap attached that can be fired by remote control if we attempt a double-cross.

'When you're satisfied that the Velazquez is genuine, we come back here, get the other suitcase, put it in the Mini, and then go back to the café and wait for fifteen minutes, to let them get clear with the money. Then we can call the police, and an Army bomb expert to defuse the booby-trap—and the painting is ours!'

Harrison, looking puzzled, muttered, 'How can I examine the Velazquez if I can't touch it?'

'You'll have to trust to your eyes, Charles. Personally, I'm beginning to doubt the whole thing. My guess is that the Velazquez isn't there at all, and there's no booby-trap to defuse; and once you and I have been sent safely off to the other side of this place, they'll drive off with the Mini and half the ransom.

'What they don't know is that Foy already knows which car it is, and they won't get through his cordon. That's what I fear, Charles. Because I don't give a damn whether Foy catches them or not. All that matters to me is getting the picture back—and I doubt if I shall.'

There was a whisper from the rear. 'Okay, sir. It's all going through to Mr Foy. Good luck.'

'Come on, Charles,' he said. 'I think we're on a stumer. But let's go over to see.'

To his surprise, the black furniture van was there. Bullen glanced at the number plate. It checked.

He raised himself on the small step at the back of the van to put the key in the lock. It went right in—and turned, and turned. It was not the key for that lock. Bullen stepped down again, wondering whether to double back to the Mini in the hope of catching them.

Harrison asked, 'What's this, then?'

He was pointing to the bottom of the left-hand door of

the van, where was chalked, 'Key fits blue van UUF 974C.'

Just to give them more time, thought Bullen angrily. But what else to do, except look for the blue van?

He glanced quickly up and down the vast lorry park. Trucks and vans were pulling out all the time, making for the exit road; a few more were coming in. From the café, drivers were coming in pairs, lighting cigarettes, making ready for the next leg of the journey. It was starting to rain.

'I think we're being conned,' he told Harrison. 'But all we can do is try to find this blue van. Start searching from this end. You take the rear three rows, I'll take the front three. I don't think we'll see this mythical blue van. But if either of us does, give a shout.'

Inside the café, an elderly van driver finished his mug of sweet tea, wiped his drooping moustache, and said to his mate, 'Come on then, Joe. We're a half-hour behind already.'

Joe stuffed the last few egg-soaked chips into his mouth, and followed reluctantly.

The driver unlocked the cabin of his black furniture van (registration ARU 125B), started the engine and began to edge out into the line of trucks and vans making for the exit road.

The policeman peering from the Bentley saw the tall top of the black furniture van moving and said urgently to his microphone, 'Black van moving off, sir.'

Foy, from control, switched to the three police cars of the striking force which were now rapidly nearing the service station; the first, he hoped, already entering the car park. 'Black van is moving off. Get the green Mini. Arrest anyone acting suspiciously. The two others cars, take the black furniture van, registration ARU 125B, at the exit road.'

'Will do, sir.' 'Entering car park now, sir. Have spotted Mini, unattended.' 'Will do, sir.'

Foy rapidly to the rest of the cordon. 'Close in on the service station with all speed.' As they went, he gave them details of what was happening.

The other man who saw the black furniture van moving was Dell. He stepped out of the Jaguar at once, gesturing to Sebastian. 'Come.'

'What's up?'

'Tell you later,' muttered Dell as they walked along the rows of parked cars among the small groups of people making for the café. He paused at a corner from which he could look back unobtrusively along the back row of cars.

'What's up?' demanded Sebastian again. 'God damn it, man, what's gone wrong?'

'Nothing, I hope. If Bullen hasn't talked to the police, we're all right. But there's always the chance that he has . . .'

Sebastian turned, started to move quickly back the way they had come, almost running. Dell caught his arm and held him. 'Take it easy, now.'

'Let's get back to the car, grab half the money, and get out.'

Sebastian's voice was rising. One or two of the passers-by, Dell saw, had turned their heads in momentary curiosity; but then walked on again.

He gripped Sebastian's arm tightly enough to make him grunt with pain.

'Stand still,' ordered Dell in a sharp whisper. 'If you run, and there are any police around, we're finished. Stand still . . . That's better. Now then, there's been a small bit of bad luck. I don't think it's going to matter. If Bullen hasn't been to the police, it can't matter . . .'

At that moment he saw a car twist suddenly into the

approach road from the motorway, jerk to a halt. Three men got out and moved rapidly towards the Mini.

Dell turned Sebastian in the direction of the café entrance. 'Do exactly what I tell you. No questions, no panic. Walk slowly with me. Make it look as though we're having an ordinary conversation.'

He kept his grip on his arm, almost pushing him slowly in the direction of the café. As they got near it, Dell could see Frosso's face through one of the windows. He motioned quickly with his head and saw that she had got it at once and was now leaving. Good girl!

The moment's distraction had loosened his hold on Sebastian. He felt him turn to look back, then stiffen; then try once more to run—this time towards the café. He had seen the men around the Mini.

Dell gripped him again, just in time to stop him. 'Walk, man. Walk.' Dell suddenly realized that the man was drugged, and the sedation had been jerked off by the shock. 'Listen to me. We've got one chance to get away. It'll be perfectly all right if you do exactly what I say. Don't run. Don't panic. I'm now going to let go of your arm. You will walk beside me, slowly and calmly, until we get to the blue van. There's no risk if you do that. If you run, they'll have us within minutes.'

He released Sebastian's arm. There was a moment of hesitation—then Sebastian started to walk slowly in the direction in which he was pointed.

'That's the way,' murmured Dell. He could cope with the fellow later. Just now, the essential was to keep him inside the margin of hysteria until they were away.

Frosso was already standing by the van when they reached it. He saw that her eyes were bright with excitement. 'What's happened?'

'Get in, quick.'

Dell took the wheel. The exit queue, which had been held up by a hubbub at the outlet to the motorway, was now moving. A man was waving the lorries through. 'Come on, get moving. Keep going. This is the police. Keep going.'

They passed the black furniture van, hauled off on to the roadside, with a couple of police gripping the startled driver and his mate, Joe, both protesting wildly, what the hell was it all about then? 'Shut up,' snapped one of the policemen.

More police cars were rushing up, gathering round the van. One came swiftly down from the other end. 'We've got the Mini. The money's still there.'

From one of the cars a man was radioing through to Foy. More cars arriving. Easing his aching limbs, the policeman was climbing out of the boot of Bullen's Bentley. A couple of uniformed men took over traffic control. 'Come on now, keep moving. Never mind what's up. Come on, get going.'

Dell took the blue van out in the middle of the queue. Once they were clear, he chose the middle lane, medium fast, making for Junction 16.

'What happened?' repeated Frosso.

'The bastard had the police there, all round us. That was what I was taking precautions against. But I really thought, up to then, that he was playing it straight, to get his picture back . . . Bastard!'

'Did they identify us?' asked Sebastian, his voice still high with near-hysteria.

'No. But no thanks to you. If I'd let you run, they'd have been on us in a moment.'

'Sebastian ran?' asked Frosso.

'He'd have run like a rabbit into a snare, if I hadn't caught him by the arm and held him.'

'You chickened?' she asked Sebastian coldly.

'Shut up, can't you? For God's sake, you weren't out there, in the open, with the police all round the Mini. All right, I chickened. I've not got the experience of your heroic friend.'

'You were told not to use drugs,' cut in Dell.

She stared at him for a moment, then turned her head towards Hugh in the driving seat. 'You were telling us what happened.'

'I'd covered us up all round,' he said. 'The money was to be put in the Mini, but we were going to take it away in the Jag, which hadn't been mentioned. Same with the vans. It was possible that, if he had the police there, they would jump the van directly Bullen knew of it. So I directed him to the wrong van.'

'We had only one there—this one.'

'Sure. So I directed him to a black furniture van that happened to pull in when I was making the arrangements. If the police jumped the van that Bullen went to, they'd get somebody's load of furniture. On the back of that van I chalked the number of this one, reckoning that was a smaller risk—and we had to take some risk.

'But then the damnedest thing happened. Most long-distance drivers and their mates take at least an hour's break for food. The bloody couple I picked on took only forty minutes. So they moved away. Bullen must have had some means of passing information to the police, who were all round. The moment that van moved, they jumped it—and jumped the Mini.

'Of course, directly I saw the furniture van moving, I got this half-wit out of the Jag, ready to get away if we had to. If the police weren't there, all we had to do was go back to the Jag and wait. But if they were, we had our own van waiting, which Bullen hadn't yet found . . .'

He swung off the motorway on to the exit to the west and sighed his relief. 'That's better. I was expecting them to come after us all the time. If Bullen reached the black van before it pulled out, he has the number of our van too. Once he gets that to the police . . .'

He pulled up sharply in the lane where Sebastian's old van was standing. It took only a few minutes to transfer the Velazquez, fixing it once more in the frame behind the Italian oil. Then they set off again.

'You drive,' Dell told Sebastian. 'Make for Daventry. From there, you and Frosso take the train to London. I'll take the van and the painting.

'Don't make any further contact tonight. Meet at Chelsea tomorrow, at eight, as usual.'

On the station platform Sebastian began to justify himself. 'All right, my nerve went, and I gave myself a shot. So what? I'm no hero—never pretended to be. And we got through all right.'

'Thanks to Hugh.'

'Nothing's lost. We've still got the Velazquez.'

'Hugh has,' she pointed out.

Sebastian stared at her, starting to tremble with rage. 'He wouldn't be such a bastard . . .'

'Maybe not. But I wouldn't count on that.'

The train was arriving at the station. Just before they got into a carriage, Sebastian took hold of her arm. 'He can't get away with that. We know too much. He wouldn't dare try.'

'And if he did,' she asked, 'what would you do, eh? What would you do, Sebastian?'

He got into the train without replying. The carriage was full, so they could not talk any more. From the seat opposite him, Frosso contemplated the frown on his face. He was, she thought, probably right. He was too deeply in for Hugh to be able to cut him out of it now. But if he did—what could Sebastian do?

Foy's car sped up to the service station, the driver pulling up sharply when he saw the black furniture van on the verge surrounded by police, two men being questioned, the straggle of police cars all round, and officers trying to untangle the traffic chaos behind, waving the stream of trucks through.

Foy stepped out in time to hear the questioning police demanding, 'Now then, where's the picture?' And the elderly driver, stubborn of face, indignant, replying, 'What bloody picture? What's the bloody idea, then? What's up—are you all bloody daft?'

'It's not in the van?' asked Foy.

'Don't think so, sir. But it's so stuffed with furniture that we can't be sure without emptying it. And there is this possibility of a booby-trap.'

Foy was turning towards the van driver when there was a commotion behind him. Police were holding up a man trying to get through.

'Let him pass,' he called. It was Bullen.

'Not that van, Foy. That was just a cover. The number of the real van's chalked on the back of this one.' He pointed to the message. 'Blue van, UUF 974C.' He held out the key.

Foy to Madge: 'Stop any van entering or leaving the park.'

Madge ran off. Foy was already assembling a team of twelve police. 'That's the registration number we're looking for. The van may not be blue. They may even have changed the number-plates by this time. So you, Jenkins, try this key on the rear door of every locked van in this park. If it fits, grab the driver and anyone else in it. Take it carefully, they may be armed. Shout out, and we'll all come.'

A sergeant reported: 'We've got the Mini, sir. The suitcase is still there, and the notes. No other obvious identification. I've circulated the number, but it's probably false, and the car stolen.'

'Never mind now,' snapped Foy, irritably for him.

He was striding over to the patrol car. 'Get through to Northampton. Patrols on the motorway, north and south, watching for this van. More patrols on the nearby roads. Not that it's likely to yield anything,' he muttered to Bullen. 'If they got out of the park, they could be off the motorway and on either the A5 or the A6 by now. I can't hold up all the traffic between London and the north. Holding up this park is bad enough.' He uneasily eyed the groups of angry, gesticulating, protesting drivers, and the long queue building up outside.

Madge came back, reporting from the search party. 'No sign of the van yet, sir. And no lock that the key fits.'

Not long after there came a call from his control car. 'Message from Northampton, sir. Blue van No. UUF 974C found empty in a lane near the approach road to the motorway at Junction 16.'

Foy got back into his car. 'Close it down,' he told Madge. 'Every car proceeds independently to base.'

A sergeant came up. 'Driver of the furniture van is, er, cutting up a bit rough, sir.'

'Tell him to make any complaint officially to the Yard.'

'Now what?' asked Bullen.

'Have to wait until they move again, I'm afraid. What's so galling is that they must in fact have been here. And we must have waved them through the cordon—the men, the vehicle, the painting, everything.'

CHAPTER XIV

Most of the day Sebastian lay in bed, smoking cigarette after cigarette, not eating anything, occasionally swallowing a neat gin. All the time, Frosso's question nagged at him: 'If he did, what would you do, Sebastian?'

At times a spasm of rage seized him, in which he silently screamed to himself that he would kill the man. When the spasm ended, he was shaken by the fierceness of it—and the stupidity. He should be deciding what he actually could do, not dissipating himself in fantasies.

Think calmly. If Dell had taken the painting, it could be only in order to cut Frosso and Sebastian himself out of it, and collect the whole ransom. How would he do it? He would probably want to use him to make fresh contact with Bullen. He would need to keep Frosso in until the last moment, so as to know what was happening through Crosby's. So Sebastian need not fear the double-cross—or even, he shuddered to himself, the violence—until whatever scheme Dell would now propose were nearly at fruition.

So not until then ought Sebastian to try anything but compliance. It was at this last moment that, if he could, he should betray Dell, and extricate Frosso and himself with at least a large part of the ransom; he conceded that he might have to lose some of it in bargaining with Bullen, to accomplish the betrayal.

In the early evening he got out of bed, shaved and started to dress. He had not opened the shop all day, but it was often shut for days at a time. Nobody would notice that.

He went over to the pub and ordered a large gin-and-mixed, nodding to Alice over the bar, but retiring with his drink to a table in the recess by the door; Alice was a talkative girl, and Sebastian did not want to chatter. He still wanted to brood. Indeed, the whole atmosphere of the pub began to jar as it gradually filled with regulars, grunting greetings to each other, each buying his own drink, cautious of getting into a school. After a second drink, he excused himself and left. As he went out, he heard one remark to another, 'What's upset Hurley, then? Not usually like that.'

At once Sebastian cautioned himself. To attract at that time even the most casual curiosity from his acquaintances might, should the police come round asking, be a small pointer in his direction. He muttered a curse at himself and went back to the shop.

Frosso was the first to arrive, but Dell came in so soon after that Sebastian had no time to say anything to her of his fears.

'Where's the painting?' he asked Dell.

Dell swivelled a thumb towards the window. Going across, Sebastian saw his old van parked at the kerb.

Mollified, Sebastian turned back into the room. Dell, without asking, was helping himself to a scotch.

He handed Sebastian the keys of his van. 'The back's locked up safely. I shouldn't shift the picture until dusk —or even leave it in the van all night.'

'Couldn't risk that.'

Dell laughed. 'I doubt if anyone is likely to steal that van. But please yourself. What we've got to do is discuss a general line for the future, and fast. The less we three are together now, the better.'

Sebastian was so elated by the realization that, as Dell had returned the painting, all his fears were needless, that he listened dutifully to what he was saying.

'I've been trying to work out just how Bullen got the police there, and how they could spring the trap so quickly. Guesswork, of course . . .'

'You don't need to guess,' said Frosso. 'I got it all at the office this morning. Charles was so full of it that he had to tell it three times, once to each of the partners. Bullen was in touch by phone with the Chief Superintendent at the Yard all the time we were approaching him. For the actual performance yesterday there was a policeman in the boot of Bullen's car, in radio touch with the Superintendent following at a distance, with several other police cars all round.'

Dell nodded. 'It had to be that. But there was no way of knowing.'

'You could have taken it into account, though,' said Sebastian—but mildly.

'I did. That was the reason for having the Jaguar standing by the Mini, and for sending Bullen first to the wrong van. And I would point out to you that it worked. We got our warning in time to get out and bring the picture with us.

'If I had directed Bullen straight to the right van, we would certainly have been jumped the moment we went to the Mini to pick up the money. And I'm not quite clear why we weren't when I went there to check on the suitcases. But that doesn't matter any more. We can turn the thing to our advantage. We've shown Bullen that he can't get the Velazquez if he works in with the police. Next time he'll have to prove to us that he's alone before we go near him.'

'How?'

'Let him sweat for a week. Today's Friday. We make no approach until Saturday of next week. Then you phone him again. I'll give you the material to make it clear to him that if he tries any more nonsense, the picture goes for ever.

'Now, I'm off. Meet here again today week, same time. Frosso, wait a little before you leave to go home

Then don't come near here again until next Friday. Sebastian, keep things absolutely normal—the shop and all that. You've both got my phone number. But don't try to get into touch with me, or with each other, unless there's a real emergency.'

'Such as . . .?'

'Such as a policeman asking questions,' said Dell, going out.

Sebastian looked at the girl. In his relief at knowing that the painting was there, and Hugh was not trying a double-cross—not yet, anyhow—he felt immensely happy. Partly, he admitted to himself, that was the quantity of gin he had drunk during the day.

'Stay the night.'

She moved away from his arm. 'Hugh said the less we're together the better—the three of us.'

'The hell with Hugh. Darling, it's been a long time.' He caught up with her. She responded indifferently to his kiss. 'At least you can stay an hour or two.'

She gripped his wrist, digging her nails into it, moving it away from her.

'Oh, come on, Frosso. Come to bed. Why not?'

'I don't want to. Not in the mood. I'm going now. This day week, here, the meeting.'

He caught hold of her as she was making for the door, swung her round, fumbling with her dress. She strained away from him, pushing his face away with the palm of her hand. 'Stop it. Do you hear? Just because you're drunk . . .'

He released her suddenly. 'Not drunk. And if that's how you feel . . .'

'Good night,' she said.

He carefully turned his back on her as she went, reached across the junk on the table for the gin bottle, poured himself another. The hell with her. She'd come round in time. He was certain of that. But he needed her tonight. After the tension of the past two days, then its sudden release, he needed her. Or perhaps he only needed a woman. Perhaps he should go to the club in the Fulham Road and pick up one of the others. He needed it, to celebrate the return of the Velazquez.

After a gulp at his glass, he shifted across to the window, to look down gratefully at the van parked by the kerb. Perhaps he'd celebrate by hanging the Velazquez on his wall for the night; it was exquisite enough in itself for an orgasm.

Turning his head, he glanced up the street towards the King's Road. Frosso had nearly reached the corner. Then he saw there was a man waiting for her. She took his arm, reached up to kiss him.

Suddenly he understood that it was Hugh.

In his choking anger, Sebastian slammed the glass down so hard on the window ledge that it smashed in his hand, cut his palm, the gin smarting as it spilled with the blood. Cursing, he lurched towards the bathroom for iodine, a plaster, thrusting his hand under the cold tap, fearful that there might be a splinter of glass.

The bitch. The sodding little bitch. So—she wasn't in the mood. He ought to have understood long ago, he told himself angrily, that she was having it off with that bastard. How long, then? From the night she moved out into that flat, he supposed.

He had stuck the plaster across his palm, staunching the blood; the cut was only slight. Now he shook his head. It was true that he was fuddled—not drunk, but a bit fuddled. He ran the cold tap into the bath, cupping the water in his uninjured hand, splashing it over his face and head. Towelling himself, he felt clearer.

That was when the implication struck him—if those two were bedding down together, they could be conspiring together. It could be that, if Dell intended to cut him out of the thing at the last moment, cheat him of his share, he would have Frosso's help. He would be needed to re-establish contact with Bullen. But when his usefulness was over, they'd ditch him, the two of them.

Well, now that he knew—now that, at a lucky moment, he had happened to glance out of the window and seen them come together at the corner—he could play his own game.

The first thing would be to hide the painting somewhere else. He must think of an alternative hiding place. That would need his brain to be clearer. It must no longer, of course, be in the shop. He knew of one or two places which could give it sanctuary. Then he would have re-established his former trump position.

He went down and unlocked the van, carefully lifting out the battered old frame with its Italian oil as camouflage, carrying it into his shop, locking the door behind him. Tomorrow he would hide the *Venus*. Tonight she should hang on the wall opposite his bed.

He turned the frame round. The wooden clips were open. In a frenzy he tugged at the stretcher, breaking a corner of the frame in the agony of getting it out, refusing to believe it—until the canvas came back, and there was only the Italian scene, the tawdry mountains, the vulgar nymphs. It was then he saw the scrap of paper stuck to the back, with a few words typed on it: 'It'll be safer in my keeping.'

Now the frenzy left Sebastian. Now he was quite sober, freezingly calm. Now he began to perceive what he was going to do. There was even, for a moment, a thin smile around his mouth. The essential now was to do the pair of them, the man and the girl—to get them both into it together. He thought he was beginning to perceive the way.

CHAPTER XV

There were times when the sense of futility against which Bullen was always struggling almost overwhelmed him; David's glum days, as his mother used to call them. All that weekend, as there was no approach from the thieves of the *Venus Revealed*, his despondency deepened. He tried to assuage it by engaging himself in the problems of the Trust—although there he touched on the very fount of his gloom. Instead of the expansion on which he had counted, there must now be long months, perhaps years, of begging for charitable money even to maintain what already existed; at the most, to bring the Birmingham house into operation, perhaps opening it two years hence.

On Monday morning he sat in his small office at the top of the Battersea building, trying to concentrate on the problems that lay on his desk. But in the mist of his eyes he could see, as always, the gaunt ruins of shattered cities, and in his nostrils smell the remembered stench of decay from a holocaust that nobody had had time to clear or level. On the day he had first driven into Hamburg, shortly after the end of the fighting, his impulse had been to end his own life. There seemed, that day, no possibility of remaining both alive and sane. But as he had forced himself to go on, to search for human contact among the rubble of other German cities, and especially in Berlin—where the horrors of the Red Army's assault were newly graven on the faces of the survivors, mostly the women—he had come to feel ever more strongly that his life must be used to make some kind of recompense. Then he had gone to Hiroshima on an Allied mission. He had not, of course, been a crew member of the Hiroshima sortie, but he allowed himself no comfort from that, no excuse. Hiroshima was merely the extension of what he himself had done through the long years of the war in Europe. He was as personally guilty of Hiroshima as of all the rest.

He closed his eyes for a moment, then returned to the case notes on his desk. The Symes family. He knew, of course, that Len Symes's 'work' in London—his occasional stint as a labourer on a building site—was only a thin cover for his chief occupation. Len was a small-time burglar. Rose Pearson had contacts with several officers of the London probation service. There was little she could not find out about any of the guests. Len had a moderately long record. If he were sent down again, it could well be for a long stretch. That would force his wife, Mary, back on her old game—not prostitution, she had got away from that years before, even before she married Len—but shop-lifting. She too had a record; and there was more than a suspicion that she had once taken the two children with her, teaching them the game.

Bullen made a wry face. Were these the people he should be helping, when so many honest families were in as deep a distress? But then he straightened in his chair. Yes, of course they were. Beneath the rubble mountains of Berlin, Cologne, Hamburg and all the rest lay the bodies of criminals alongside honest men, of whores with children crushed in their arms, of thieves, rogues, blackmailers, perverts, along with the worthy citizens, good mothers, priests. All human. He was in debt to all of them.

'Send the whole family to Dorset,' he had told Rose. When she objected that, she had heard, Len Symes was thought by the police to have broken into a tobacconist's and rifled the till while actually living in Sawdon House, Bullen raised his hand to silence her. 'Let's not go into that. Get them down there as soon as you can, Rose.'

So what, in the end, Bullen mused at his desk, could one do with the Symeses? Could the help ever be more than stopgap? And was that of any value? The Symeses would never get anywhere permanent to live.

Bullen sighed. He did not deceive himself; in the end there was no solution. All he could do was go blindly on, take people in without questions, never stopping to consider, to weigh the desert against the need, never judging, never discriminating. A bomb did not discriminate.

He eased his shoulders, frowned, shook himself. He had thought to have outgrown, recently, these moods of deep despond. It was, of course, the despair of ever now getting back the Velazquez. How much he could have done with that money! Now he was convinced that the hope of ever seeing the painting again was small. He should have followed his instinct in the first place and stayed away from the police. What right had he, after all, to side with law, order, retribution for crime?

Rose returned with the second post of the day. A few minutes later she held something out to him, asking, 'David, what's this?'

He took the manila envelope which she had slit at the top. But before emptying it, he turned it over. On the back was a figure 8, drawn with a felt pen.

Slowly, gingerly he felt inside, drawing out a plain white card on which, in some sort of stamping ink, was the print of a thumb and four fingers of a left hand.

Bullen stared at it for a moment, puzzled. Then the significance reached him. He placed the card carefully on his blotting pad and peered inside the envelope; it contained nothing else. By the postmark, it had been posted the previous afternoon in a northern district of London.

'What is it?' Rose asked.

'A set of fingerprints. I think we may be in contact again.'

'But how . . .?'

'The only indication we have is the fingerprints left on the frame in the upper room at Crosby's by the man who impersonated Charles Harrison that night and went off with the Velazquez in the morning.'

'You think this comes from him? But why should he send you that?'

'To prove he's the man who has the painting. This must be only the preliminary.' Bullen was getting excited. But then he checked himself. 'Damn! My only way of checking is to take this to the police.'

'I'm glad.'

Bullen shrugged. 'That's how we missed last week. However, there's no alternative.' He was dialling the number Foy had given him. 'Hallo, Superintendent. Bullen here. I think we're in touch again.'

He told of the envelope and the prints.

'Sounds like it, sir. I'll send an officer round straight away to collect the material. It won't take long to check. I'll ring you back. If the prints are what you suppose, you'll be getting another contact, probably by phone, within the next couple of days, I'd say. I'm relying on you to let me know directly.'

An hour after Bullen had surrendered the envelopes and the card to the officer who came for them, Foy rang him.

'You were right. He's the man.'

As it turned out, it was not a phone call. Bullen sat at his desk almost without intermission throughout the rest of Monday, and Tuesday. At Scotland Yard, Foy arranged to be informed at the moment, day or night, that the phone tap picked up another call from the man with the phoney scowse accent. But there was no call.

What arrived at Sawdon House, first post on Wednesday, was another envelope bearing the figure 8 on the reverse; this one had been posted in east London. Rose handed it to Bullen without a word.

This time it was a typed letter: 'You must have checked the prints with the police, so you know I'm the man who took the Velazquez. But don't tell them you have received this letter or bring them in in any way. I have means of knowing if you do. Last time I knew that you had a policeman in the boot of your car, in radio touch with the police cordon all round you. That's why you didn't get the painting on Thursday at the service station on the M1. I no longer have the painting. I have been swindled out of it by a man and a woman. I know who and where they are, and I'll turn them in. But I shall need enough money to get out of the country and disappear. If you pay me £50,000 in used £5 and £1 notes, two days later you'll receive the names and addresses of the people who have the painting. Take the information to the police, but make it a condition that you don't reveal how you got it. Then they can arrest the two who have your painting, and you'll get it back. It won't cost you a quarter of a million—only £50,000. It's the last chance you'll ever get of recovering the *Venus Revealed*. If you don't pay me, or if you go to the police with this letter, I shall tell the woman that the police know who she is, and the man will then at once destroy the painting. He has no scruples, and is quite indifferent to art. But if you accept my terms, which are unalterable, go tomorrow to your house in Dorset and wait for instructions.'

Bullen handed it to Rose, keeping silent while she read it. 'Well?'

'You'll send this to Mr Foy, of course.'

Bullen shook his head. 'The man, whoever he is, would know. He must have some means of knowing—

he knew there was a policeman in the boot of the Bentley. This time I'll try on my own.'

'But how will you get the £50,000? The police have all those forged notes.'

'It won't be fake,' he said, reaching for the telephone. 'What's Claridge's number? Please God Mr Hymans is still in London.'

Joe Hymans was still at Claridge's. He was convinced, after that first odd visit, that Sir David Bullen would return to him, the second time with a proposition. Joe Hymans was willing to wait a month—more if need be—to get an uncontested chance at the *Venus Revealed.*

That, to his joy, was exactly what Sir David Bullen offered him. When he arrived at Hymans's sitting-room at Claridge's, he went straight to it. 'Mr Hymans, I believe I can get the Velazquez back. You won't expect me to give you details. All I can tell you, in strict confidence, is that there seems to be a quarrel among the thieves. One of them is ready to betray the others—for a consideration. The consideration is £50,000.'

'That's a lot of money.'

'That's why I've come to you, on Harrison's recommendation, as I told you on my first visit. If I can have £50,000 in used £5 and £1 notes by tomorrow morning, there is an excellent chance that the Velazquez may be recovered. If one of your clients is prepared to risk that much, when we get the painting back I will sell it to him for £1,750,000—which is at least a quarter of a million less than every serious bidder was prepared to pay at the sale.'

Bullen watched Joe Hymans while he pretended to ponder this. A slight, short, elderly man with the sad, serious face of a scholar and the eyes of a used-car salesman.

'How much risk is there, Sir David, that the money might go and the picture not be recovered?'

'A grave risk. This is a gamble at odds, but for very high stakes.'

'How do you know that the man has the picture?'

'He hasn't—or says he hasn't. That's why he's willing to betray his associates who have, he says, double-crossed him, and who hold the painting. What we do know is that the man in touch with me is the man who impersonated Charles Harrison on the night before the sale, and took the painting away from Crosby's. He has produced proof that satisfied not only me, but the police. What we don't know is whether he is simply trying to defraud me of £50,000 or whether, if he gets it, he will in fact supply the information that will lead to the recovery of the painting. It's a desperate gamble, Mr Hymans. But it may be the only chance we shall get. The man says that, if I don't pay him, he will contrive to alarm the others so much that they will destroy the canvas.'

A long pause. Then Hymans: 'I'm not going to ask any of my clients to take that gamble, Sir David.'

'You're probably right.'

'I shall take it myself,' added Hymans softly.

Bullen smiled. 'Thank you, Mr Hymans. I have to have the notes by tomorrow morning.'

'Call on my banker tomorrow. The notes will be there. I will see to it that he alone deals with the matter.'

'Thank you again. I will tell my lawyer to send you my formal undertaking that, should the painting be recovered in the next six months, the Sawdon Trust will sell it to you for £1,175,000, which will include the £50,000 you are now advancing; and that if it is recovered at a later date, I will repay you £50,000, and give you the opportunity of making the first offer for it.'

The thin, sad old man smiled gently. 'That will be quite unnecessary, Sir David. I accept your word.'

Only an American dealer would have been shrewd

enough, and large-minded enough—and, probably, rich enough—to do that, thought Bullen; which was why they were the greatest.

It was the following morning, Thursday morning, when Syndercombe walked into Charles Harrison's office and asked, 'What's all this about helping Bullen to recover the *Venus Revealed?*'

'You know I did. And we failed.'

'I mean this second attempt. Joe Hymans has just been on the phone to me . . .'

He broke off, realizing that Harrison's secretary was in her chair at the corner of the desk, notebook out, taking dictation.

'All right, Frosso,' said Charles. 'We'll have to leave the letters for a moment.'

She gathered from the desk the letters to which she already had replies in her notebook, and managed under their cover to depress the switch on the house phone to her own desk in the office adjoining. She could listen undisturbed because, mercifully, the girl who shared the office with her was on holiday.

'I've just had Joe Hymans on the phone, asking me to thank you for sending Bullen along to him to get the £50,000.'

'What £50,000?'

Syndercombe passed his hand wearily across his distinguished forehead; he was fast beginning to wish that he had not, after all, changed his mind about resigning. 'Joe says that Bullen told him the thieves have quarrelled, and the one who impersonated you on the night the painting was stolen is now prepared, for £50,000, to betray the others, so that it may be recovered. He says you recommended Bullen to go to him to raise the cash. Hyman is putting it up, on Bullen's promise to sell him the Velazquez, when he has it back, for £1,750,000.

Hymans is overjoyed. He says he doesn't give a damn about the risk, he has a hunch it'll come off. And he's very grateful to us—to you in particular.'

'I know absolutely nothing about it. Some time ago I told Bullen that Joe Hymans was hanging around at Claridge's, hoping for a chance to get the Velazquez for himself if it were recovered. Other than that, I haven't mentioned him to Bullen, and I know nothing about any further attempt to recover the painting.'

'Hymans took it for granted that you knew.'

'Not a word, I assure you.'

'If Bullen gets it back,' said Syndercombe in a pained voice, 'he'll sell it direct to Joe. Our commission would have been at least £200,000.'

Harrison considered. 'I reckon Bullen, who's an honest man, would agree to pay us anyway.'

Syndercombe disagreed. 'He'll do anything for extra money for those damned charities of his. Not a chance.'

'I believe we could at least arrange a reasonable compromise,' Harrison persisted. 'Have you talked to Bullen?'

'No. I rang his London hostel and was told he's on his way to his Dorset place. On reflection, I'm relieved I didn't catch him. He may have a good reason for not telling us of this development. Perhaps there could be something to prejudice his chance of recovering the painting.'

'I'll go and talk to Bullen,' suggested Charles. 'I'll cook up some excuse for going down to Dorset at the weekend. I'll pretty soon find out what's happening. And I feel sure I could persuade him to be reasonable about our cut. After all, if it hadn't been for me, he wouldn't even have known that he had a valuable painting in his attic. He'll see reason.'

'Let's hope so. But be cautious. Better pretend not to know anything of this development, and don't say anything about a call from Hymans. My dear Charles, this affair has already turned my few grey hairs white. If it went wrong again, it might take years for Crosby's reputation to recover. Caution, above all.'

'I promise. Rely on me.'

When Syndercombe had gone, Harrison went to the door to Frosso's office and called her in again. She carried back the bundle of letters to replace on his desk, contriving as she did so to switch off the house phone.

She seated herself again. 'You were in the middle of your letter to Wilson, our new public relations man in Los Angeles,' she told him in her usual even, languid voice. 'I'll read you over the last paragraph.'

CHAPTER XVI

She waited until her lunch-hour before slipping away to phone Hugh, the first time she had used the number. There was no reply. She went into a pub just off New Bond Street, shouldering her way through the crowd of office people and tourists to get herself a ham sandwich and a lager beer. From the telephone booth in the corner of the saloon bar she tried the number again. Still no reply.

Slowly she walked out into the street. She knew his flat was in the Cromwell Road, but did not know where. Always they had met in her small flat in Fulham. Perhaps she could find out the address from the office of his letting agents. But instinct forbade her to do that. Anyway, if he were there, he would answer the phone. She tried twice more, from different booths, but without raising him. Then she had to return to her office; vital, now, that she should be seen doing nothing out of the usual.

It was not a busy afternoon. She typed the letters with her customary precision and coped with the few phone calls that came in. Charles returned from a business lunch very late and very jovial. The only chore he had for her was to ring Sir David's number in Dorset. Bullen himself had not yet arrived. 'It's Miss Pearson, the housekeeper, on the phone,' she told Charles.

'Put her through. Oh hallo, Miss Pearson. Charles Harrison here. I wonder if Sir David could possibly bear for me to visit him at the weekend . . . Well, I have a few points I'd like to discuss with him—yes, the obvious subject . . . Unfortunately I just missed him here in London—didn't know he was off to Dorset until after he'd gone . . . Well, I suppose he will be rather busy.' He laughed ingratiatingly. 'Aren't we all, eh, Miss Pearson . . .? Well, look here, let's leave it at that, unless Sir David rings up positively to stop me, I'll come tomorrow on the afternoon train. I won't trouble you to put me up, I know how full the Hall is. I'll get a room in the pub, just staying the one night, if Sir David can spare the time.' When he had hung up, he grunted, 'Old battleaxe!'

At last Frosso could leave, hurrying from the building, stopping at the phone booth outside the post office. 'Hallo.' She almost sobbed with relief when she heard his voice.

'I'm going straight to Fulham,' she said in a low voice. 'Meet me there as soon as you can. It's vitally urgent.'

'Right. Take a taxi.'

'No, I'll go by bus, as I do every afternoon. I'll be about half an hour.'

He was waiting in the flat when she arrived. 'Well?'

She told him of the overheard conversation between Mr Syndercombe and Charles. 'It can't be true, can it?' she asked anxiously. 'Why should Sebastian accept a much smaller sum for taking, by himself, the same sort of risks as we'd all take together—and he gets his third share? Why, Hugh? Why?

'And why should he think there's been a quarrel between us? There hasn't been. Oh, a few tiffs. He's been jealous of you, irritated at having to cut you in. I wouldn't go to bed with him after you left on Friday. But that seems scarcely enough . . . Not a real quarrel, anyway. And it's not true that we've swindled him out of the picture.'

'I didn't return it to him. I left a note in his van that it would be safer in my keeping.'

'Oh,' she murmured.

So it wasn't fantasy. Sebastian did mean to betray them. She felt a sudden shiver of terror, but of excitement too. For she saw the intent look in Hugh's eyes, his face otherwise immobile, but pale, serious, slightly frowning.

'We can stop him?' she asked hesitantly.

'Oh yes, I think so.' The man suddenly roused himself. 'Oh yes,' he repeated softly, 'I think we can stop him all right. We'll go separately to the shop. You take the Underground to Sloane Square and walk back. I'll be watching the shop. If he's in, just keep him talking. I'll wait five minutes, then come up. If he's not in, come straight out into the street again.'

'And when we find him?'

'We'll have a little talk,' said Hugh pleasantly.

There was a light in the window of the room above the shop. Frosso glanced round, but could not see Hugh. After a moment of hesitation she put her key in the lock, and went up.

The living-room had been somewhat tidied. A woman was poking about with a broom behind the chiffonier, which she had lifted out at one end from the wall; a dark, slatternly woman, no longer young, in slacks and an old cotton shirt, a brown scarf tied round her hair. She looked up with surprise. 'Who the hell may you be? And how the hell did you get in?'

'Where's Sebastian?'

'Oh, he don't live here any more. Sold the place to my man.'

'Since when?'

'Since yesterday.'

Somehow Frosso had to get out to warn Hugh, and yet be able to bring him back up again. Searching for a way, she said, 'Oh damn! He was re-making some jewellery for me. Rather expensive, it was. He arranged for me to collect it here this evening. My friend, who's waiting downstairs, is to pay for it. I wonder if he gave it to your husband?'

'Bring your friend up, then. Wilf'll be back in a few minutes. He only went over to the pub for a pint.'

'Oh, thanks,' said Frosso, turning for the door.

'And how did you get in?' asked the woman again.

Frosso gave her a tired smile. 'You'd better get Wilf to change the lock. I expect quite a few girls have a key.'

Down in the street Frosso looked around, and then Hugh was with her; he came unobtrusively, very swiftly, like a shadow. She told him. He took her arm and they went up.

The woman clearly approved of Hugh. She moved some junk to make room for them on the settee, assuring them Wilf wouldn't be long.

'They've just bought the business from Sebastian,' said Frosso, explanatory. 'Rather sudden, wasn't it?'

'I couldn't say. I don't interfere in Wilf's business affairs. He's known Mr Hurley a long time, in the way of business. Maybe they've been arranging it for a long time. I wouldn't know.'

'Any idea where he's gone?' Frosso asked.

'Abroad, I think he said. But he didn't say where.'

Wilf, who then arrived, was short, stout, ginger-haired, in corduroy trousers and a soiled shirt open at his thick neck, beneath which a lot more red hair matted. He was cheery enough, conversational, forthcoming, informative. Yes, he'd taken over the business from Sebastian Hurley. Gave him 200 nicker for the goodwill and stock, and another 300 to be paid when the assignment of the lease came through.

'Paid where?' asked Dell.

'He's going to let me know when the time comes.'

'It's just that he has this necklace of mine,' explained Frosso. 'I expect he forgot all about it, in the complication of selling the business.'

'What's it like?'

'Semi-precious stones from South Africa. More sentimental value than anything else.' She glanced at Hugh and tried a little simper.

Well, said Wilf, if he came across anything like it, in all the junk in the shop, he'd put it aside, if she'd call in again. No, Sebastian hadn't said where he was going. Got a chance to buy a villa cheap somewhere, Wilf believed, and had made rather a nice bit of money out of something or other, that he'd rather have overseas than in this country. Wilf winked. Frosso smiled understandingly. And they went.

Hugh gripped her arm and steered her quickly back to the King's Road, into a small, dark, expensive Greek restaurant. 'We have to eat. May as well, while we talk.' He gestured to the head waiter, who seemed to know him and led to a table for two in an embrasure near the back, out of earshot in all this dining din, and very nearly out of view. He quickly ordered for both of them, lifting an eyebrow towards her to get her approval. When it was served, he began, 'Where's he gone?'

Frosso shrugged. 'He would scarcely mention it to me. The idea is to give us both away, remember?'

Hugh was musing. 'How's he going to collect from Bullen? That's the question. If we knew that . . .'

Frosso put down her knife. 'Of course, that's where he's gone. Bullen has gone back to his house in Dorset.'

'You knew that, and didn't tell me?'

'Sorry,' she muttered. 'I'm not thinking straight. Hugh, I'm scared. I'm damn frightened.'

He ignored her. 'Of course that's where he has gone. I'm driving down to Dorchester tonight. You'd better come with me. It'll be easier to find him with two of us looking. How about your office?'

'Two of the secretaries share the flat I used to live in. I can ring them there tonight, say I'm ill, tell them to tell Charles tomorrow.'

'That'll do.'

'Suppose you're wrong. Suppose he hasn't gone to Dorset. If we miss him . . .'

'I'm not wrong,' he assured her. 'Bullen wouldn't have gone anywhere, once he'd received another contact—as he must have done—unless he was told to.

'Sebastian must have sent him to Dorset. That's where Sebastian hopes to collect—much easier there than in London, with all the police around. It was quite a clever move on Sebastian's part. Sebastian is learning fast.

'However, there are one or two more lessons coming to him soon.'

Because Foy had gone to Manchester, Madge had to get him on the blower. 'First break we've had, sir. Boy Shepherd has been picked up in Brighton in a stolen car. Had his girl with him. They're both being held. Shall I go?'

'Yes, go tonight. I'll be back in London tomorrow around noon.'

It was only just after ten at night when Madge sat down opposite the sullen youth in an interrogation room in Brighton police station. 'No need of an introduction,' Madge told the local sergeant. 'Boy and I are old acquaintances, eh, Boy? And he knows that when I say anything, I stick to it, eh, Boy? Now then, I'm not worried about what you've been pulled in for today. I want you to think back a bit, Boy—a little more than a couple of weeks back. It's Thursday the 22nd today. What I'm interested in is the night of Monday the 5th —sixteen days ago.'

'Don't know what you're talking about.'

Then Madge knew he was on to the right man. Boy Shepherd was only a car thief, illiterate, never got much from his schooling, lived from one petty crime to another, spent what money he had on cheap, flashy clothes and equally cheap, flashy girls, never drank much, or gambled, and quite incapable of fooling even a moderately good interrogator. At the mention of the date, the look of startled fear that came into his eyes was obvious.

'I'm not going to ask where you were, Boy, because I know where you were. There'll be a charge to face later on, Boy. Kidnapping isn't a trivial offence, you know that. Accessory to a theft of getting on for two million pounds isn't a petty offence either. But perhaps you didn't know about that, eh? That's why I'm giving you a chance.'

'You're talking daft. I don't know nothing about it.'

'About what?'

'About what you're talking about,' he uneasily replied.

So it went on, patiently, for nearly half an hour. The youth was striving to preserve his sullen surface, but he was palpitating beneath.

'I'll tell you what I want,' said Madge evenly. 'I want to know who put you on to it. I'll accept that you don't know the identity of the man with the gun. I'll accept that, Boy. I'm bending over backwards to make things easy for you, aren't I? But you must know who put you in touch, who hired you.'

'I've told you, I don't know nothing about it.'

'Was it Johnnie Wicks?' asked Madge. But that name raised no flicker in the youth's eyes. 'Or was it Gerry Phillips . . . or Harry Johnson . . .?' Patiently he went on and on, putting in all the likely or even the possible names. And at last came the flash of fear—worse than fear this time, terror, pure terror. Madge could understand that. So it was Freddie Bradford. Boy Shepherd had reason for his terror. One day the gang-busting squad at the Yard would winkle Freddie from the sidestreets of south-east London where he ruled; and whence he made his trips up west, living it up socially with a lot of wealthy, influential, even a few reputable people. But until he was cornered, any insignificant villain who crossed him, like this little car thief, could be certain of the most vicious beating, and probably worse.

Madge gazed at the youth for a long minute, almost pitying. 'Ah well, if you won't tell me,' he said at last, getting up from the table, 'I shan't be able to help you when the time comes. As it will, Boy. Don't have any doubt about that.'

When Shepherd had been put down again, Madge refused the offer of a bed for the night. It was essential to get at Freddie Bradford as quickly as possible, but that was not something that Madge could do. It needed somebody who knew Freddie, and whom Freddie knew. It needed somebody who could convince him that, this time, all they wanted was information on the quiet, and not to involve Freddie himself. That meant it would have to be done by one of the Yard specialists. On the drive back to London, Madge pondered. He had made progress. He could be sure that it was Boy Shepherd who had driven the van in which Charles Harrison was taken to the West Country on the night the painting was stolen, and probably it was he who had stolen the van and the two cars used in the attempt to collect the ransom at the service station on the M1; after a few days, a Jaguar had been reported as abandoned in the park there and, since it had been stolen, had probably been intended as the getaway car.

So with Boy Shepherd they had made the first breakthrough, taken the first pace towards the identity of the thieves. But, Madge gloomily pondered, it had brought them straight away up against Freddie Bradford. He wished it had been almost anybody else.

As there was no safe at Sawdon Hall, Bullen shoved under his bed the case containing the £50,000 he had collected that morning from the American bank. He did not bother to lock the door of his room. He was the last person at Sawdon Hall whom any of the guests would suspect of having anything worth stealing.

He sat for hours by the phone after dinner, reading. There was no call. On the Friday morning he rose early, but did not take his customary walk to the river and back over the downs. He stayed by the phone, asking for breakfast to be brought to his office on a tray, pretending pressure of work. But all that morning there were only the usual calls on Sawdon Trust business. Rose dealt with them.

By lunchtime Bullen was getting anxious. Should he have told the police when he received the letter? Perhaps it could have led them to someone. Was it merely a ruse to get him out of London?

Depression began to settle on him again. He was aware of the early symptoms of what had at one time threatened to be a nervous collapse, and which he thought he had overcome some years before. David's glum days. He smiled sadly at the euphemism, so characteristic of his mother. After lunch, having told Rose to send for him immediately if there were a phone message, he went through the crowded dormitory quarters of the house to the private door into the old wing, to see his mother; as he had been accustomed to, years before, on his glum days.

Lady Mary Bullen was seated in a small arm-chair by the french window that was open on to the rose garden; but she would not step out through it, she never did. Bullen dimly understood that so long as the rose garden was there to be looked at, it confirmed his mother's belief that her world, the world she had known, existed as always beyond; but if she stepped into it and looked beyond—what would she see?

'Ah, David,' she greeted him, smiling, turning in the chair towards him. He kissed her gently, then sat on the low stool opposite her chair. It was astonishing how young she still looked. She was well into her seventies, but with a figure as slender as when she had been a young wife, and a face untroubled by the cares of the world—for the actual world had not existed for her since the sudden, frantic, brain-muddling grief when his father had been killed. She had not exactly retained the world of the nineteen-tens. She was aware that time flowed by and that she herself was old. It was rather that she had created a world of three delicately-furnished rooms looking on to a rose garden, in which there was no anxiety, no grief. The dresses she wore were not in the style of any decade, but vaguely suggesting difference.

'One of my glum days,' he said.

She put out her hand, softly to stroke the back of his. 'You should marry, David. You can't spend all your life as a bachelor in London, living in your club. You must settle, my dear. You should marry.'

He smiled. There was no point in reminding her that

he was already married. She had long forgotten all about Sarah. For his mother, he was still the young squire, who must soon abandon his easy bachelor life in London and, for the sake of the estate, settle down and marry. 'Perhaps, one day,' he placated her, 'or perhaps not. It isn't important.'

'But it is. The tenants need an heir.'

'There's cousin Simon.'

She made a little movement of distaste. 'That side of the family . . .'

If she learned that there was no longer any need of an heir, nothing much to inherit—all given over into the Trust, in perpetuity—her life would end. But there would be no point in destroying something so placid, so gentle.

'That girl, Rose Pearson, whom you bring to see me sometimes—she's in love with you.'

'Yes, I know, Mother.'

'Of course, she's not from our part of the county. But I dare say . . .'

He smiled again, stood up to go, kissed her forehead. 'Thank you, darling,' he said. 'You've done me good. The day feels not quite so glum.'

Back in his office he waited still for some indication; but there was nothing.

Rose asked, 'Do you think the letters were a hoax?'

'Couldn't have been. The fingerprints proved that. I can't think of any reason why the man should want me out of London, except to get in touch with me to pick up the money. But there was nothing yesterday, and so far nothing today. I suppose I must face that we shan't get the painting back. I ought to be making contingency plans——what to cut.'

'Cancel the contract for the Birmingham house. Luckily you've only put down the deposit, nothing exchanged yet. Stop taking people in here, or at Battersea, without payment. You know the original idea was that they should all pay modest rents. And you simply don't charge.'

'The lawyers were doubtful about it,' he weakly excused.

'Oh, rubbish, David. You're being too soft, that's all.' The phone rang. She picked it up. 'Sawdon Hall office . . .' She listened for a moment then, without a word, handed the phone to Bullen.

'Sir David? Good. Do you have the money?'

It was the unmistakable scowse accent again.

'Yes, I have it.'

'Put it in a suitcase. At ten o'clock tonight take it in your car to Sawdon Abbas, turn right at the post office on to the coast road. Three miles along there's an old quarry. I expect you know it.'

'Of course.'

'Just inside the entrance there's a disused wooden hut. The door is open—I forced it last night. Put the case inside the hut—you'll need a flashlight. Close the hut door and return to your house—and don't leave it again until tomorrow morning, after breakfast. And don't try anything this time. If you try to spring any sort of trap, I shall know. Then I shall take the necessary steps to alarm the people who have the painting, and they will at once destroy it. You'll never hear from any of us again.'

'I'm not in touch with the police or anybody else. You have my word.'

'Better not be. If I get the money safely, you will receive, in the first post at Sawdon Hall on Monday, the names and addresses you want. After that you can do whatever you like—call in the police, anything. I shall no longer be around.'

The usual click, pause, purr of the dialling tone.

'Don't go,' urged Rose, tense.

'There's no risk. I shan't be away for more than half an hour.'

'If you are, nothing will stop me ringing the police.'

He stood beside her, patted her arm. 'Calm down now, my dear.'

'I mean it, David,' she declared vehemently. 'I mean it.'

CHAPTER XVII

By mid-morning Frosso felt exhausted. First there had been the night drive from London to Dorchester, then a restless night in a pub. Now all morning she had been walking round the town in hot sun, from one lodging-house to another, pretending to look for a room, but always searching for any trace of Sebastian, trying to identify him by innocent-seeming questions about the other guests. Hugh was doing the same in the hotels and pubs.

They met at eleven in the saloon bar of the King's Arms. Hugh raised his eyebrows questioningly at her, but she shook her head. 'No sign of him.' She took with gratitude the glass of cold lager.

'If not here, then where?' mused Dell. 'He wouldn't dare go to Sawdon Abbas itself, or any of the surrounding villages. A stranger stands out too much in a village.'

The idea came to her. 'It's the holiday season. Isn't that the obvious thing? Hide in the seaside holiday crowds?'

'Weymouth?'

'Of course. It's not all that far from Bullen's place.'

'Drink up and come on.'

She sighed and followed him.

They were there in twenty minutes. Dell put his big

Rover into a crowded park near the promenade. 'Better not split up this time. We'd lose each other. Walk separately, but stay in sight of me. If either of us spots him, beckon.'

She turned on to the sands, threading through the noisy, sun-reddened holiday-makers, huddles of them stretched out flat in the sunshine, children with buckets and spades splashing along the water's edge, the small waves of the receding tide curling gently on to the wet smoothness of the beach, a tanker putting out from the harbour mouth, laden motorboats taking trips round the bay, gulls screaming overhead, the smells of ice-cream, suntan oils, sweat, and the seaweedy aroma of the sea. Every so often she glanced to her right to ensure that she could still see Hugh making his way through the crowds on the esplanade itself.

For half an hour they trudged the length of the front, but never a sight of Sebastian. She grew more and more aware of hopelessness. It would be easy to have passed him in this throng, or for him to have stepped from the town on to the beach just after she and Hugh had gone by. Dispirited, she looked at her watch. It was nearly one o'clock. She turned off the beach on to the roadway. Hugh stopped expectantly, but she shook her head. 'It'd be a fluke if we saw him in this lot. I need food, and even more I need a drink. That looks a reasonable hotel across the way . . .'

He bought her a large gin-and-tonic, after which she felt better. He ordered lobster, green salad, a half-bottle of Piesporter '69 to drink with it. They said no more about Sebastian until they could get out of the packed, stifling restaurant on to an open terrace for coffee.

'There must be a better way than chance encounter,' she said.

'How? In a town like this there are too many hotels and boarding-houses for just the two of us to cover. He's probably using a fake name.'

Then she had it. 'He must have a car. It wouldn't be feasible without a car.'

'He has his old van.'

'No, it was still standing outside the shop yesterday. He must have sold it with the business.'

'He wouldn't have the nerve to steal one,' murmured Dell, 'nor, really, any need. So he hires one in London and drives here. How does that help?'

'If that's what he did, it doesn't. But suppose he took a train from London and hired a car in Weymouth. He'd have to use his real name, because he'd have to produce his driving licence.'

'Certainly worth a try.'

The few self-drive car-hire firms were listed in the yellow pages of the telephone directory. Frosso took the job on, walking from one to the other. 'Please could you help me? I'm looking for my fiancé. He's down here on a short holiday, and I thought I couldn't get away from my office. But the boss relented, and I have four days. And I don't know where he's staying. But he said he would be hiring a self-drive car. Hurley, his name is—Sebastian Hurley.' The softness of her pleading glance overcame the doubts.

At the third garage she located him.

When he left the stuffy booth in the post office, after telephoning to Bullen, Sebastian wandered out into the sunshine, feeling good. He had no doubt now of the £50,000. Bullen would certainly be able to put up that much. It would be in the quarry hut by half past ten that night at latest. Sebastian would collect it at about eleven.

So he had more than seven hours to wait. How would he get through them? He could not face sitting them out in the frowsty private hotel at the back of the town where he had taken a room. Nor did he want to drive about the Dorset countryside. To hell with countryside; he was a man for towns. And suppose, by some irony, he were caught in a car accident, at this very last moment, with the fortune waiting for him that night. No motoring!

He wandered through the town in the direction of the sea. He would keep his side of the bargain with Bullen. Too right he would! He could send him Dell's phone number, and put him on to Frosso. Sebastian found the idea most agreeable. Once the pair of them were caught, he would be able to follow their retribution in the newspaper. There would be some kind of English-language newspaper available, wherever he ended up.

That he had not quite decided. But the first jump was all that really mattered, and that was arranged. He had the train and boat tickets to Ireland. It would be just as easy to lose himself in Dublin as in London. Then, at leisure, he could arrange for the onward journey. Luckily he already had a spare passport in a false name. That had been part of his preparation for getting away when they picked up the ransom. Freddie had told him how to get the passport. It was ridiculously easy. All you needed was a copy of the birth certificate of somebody else of about your own age; and this the authorities themselves provided, no questions asked, for a few pence. Then you faked signatures of a clergyman and a Justice of the Peace. Freddie had warned him that there were spot checks, but they were infrequent. The chances of being discovered were very small. And the thing worked. He had the passport.

He found a seat on the esplanade and loosened his necktie, took off his jacket. It was hot in the sunshine. The panorama of the beach delighted him. Every year, when he was a child, his parents had taken him for a summer holiday to just such a beach—usually to Bournemouth. In his euphoria, he allowed himself a sentimental recollection of his childhood. How bright, how promising, life had then seemed! How unsordid! A fair-haired boy of about eight years of age was building a sandcastle on the beach just before him, watched by a prim young couple sitting on deckchairs, the picnic basket at the woman's side. It might easily have been himself and his parents, all those years ago, Sebastian lazily amused himself by imagining.

The child, tiring of the sandcastle, ran off down the beach to lower himself on to the wet sand where little waves broke over him. The whimsical notion came to Sebastian that he too would bathe in the sea—something he had not done for at least twenty-five years. He smiled at the thought of joining this harmless holiday scene, as though he were rejoining his own youth. Absurd, of course, but the idea nevertheless delighted him. And he had all those hours to get through. Rising from the seat, he wandered back into the town, found an outfitter's shop and bought a pair of bathing trunks and a towel; he chose the most vividly-coloured trunks he could find, chuckling with amusement at it all.

The towel was big enough for him to undress beneath it on the beach. The sea was warm and gentle, caressing; he found that he had not quite forgotten how to swim.

When he emerged, he spread the towel on the sand and lay for a long time sunning himself, drowsing, even for a while sleeping. After he woke, he looked pleasurably round at the recumbent sunbathers on the beach. Close by him a little blonde lay face downwards, sleeping. Her dress, shoes and tights were neatly placed by her head. She had unhooked the back of the bra of her bikini, and the side of one small, firm, bronzed breast was in Sebastian's view. He smiled appreciatively. But such delights were not for that particular day. There would be women in plenty, but only in the future, once he had the money and was safely away.

Many of the sunbathers, he now noticed, were rising from the sands, gathering their belongings and leaving in groups. Of course—that most English of all holiday components, high tea. Sebastian glanced at his watch. Half past five. He suddenly recalled from his youth, with astonishing clarity, the smell of fried eggs, and kippers, and the delicate aroma of shrimps. He grinned to himself. High tea! He wriggled back into his clothes, wrapped the towel in a roll around the bathing trunks, and set off back into the town. There was a big café. There was a huge set tea and, for an extra charge, fresh shrimps. He sat there peeling them, popping the tiny pink bodies into his mouth. The flavour was less tangy than he had remembered, but the sensation was exquisite.

He spun the tea out until the pubs were open. Because he would need to drive, he allowed himself only two large gins-and-tonic. Then he set off to walk back to his shabby hotel. He would rest for three hours, and then would come the action. Whether Bullen would get his picture back Sebastian did not care. All that he counted on was that Dell and Frosso would be trapped. The sentences would be long, he could depend on that.

He walked dreamily along the rather long, empty road, at the far end of which his hotel stood. As he passed a saloon car parked by the kerb, the door opened, a hand grabbed his wrist, he was jerked against the side of the car. He could feel, in his paralysis of terror, the point of a knife pricking his belly.

'All right, Sebastian,' said Dell. 'Get in.'

Frosso, who was driving, followed the road which Hugh had traced for her on the Ordnance Survey map he had bought that afternoon. It led across one of the moors that are scattered over Dorset, that lovely, not thickly populated county, the Hardy country. There were sounds of struggle in the back of the car. In the driving mirror she could just make out that Hugh had pulled Sebastian's hands behind his back and was fastening them with a thin cord. Frosso felt a touch of fright. But what alternative was there? She was in it now with Hugh. No turning back now.

'Over to the right,' came Hugh's sharp instruction from the rear. She turned the car on to what was little more than a track across the moor. 'Stop under that tree on the crest of the hill.'

When she had pulled up, she looked round at the scene in the fading light. The nearest house was at least a mile away. There was nobody in sight. Nobody could get within a mile of them without being seen. 'Keep watch,' said Hugh softly.

She was glad of the excuse not to have to look back at the two men. She had just caught a glimpse of Sebastian, hands pinioned behind him, lying back against the car cushion, miserably failing to hide his complete panic; and Hugh twisting to face him, staring at him with contempt.

'So you were going to shop us, eh Sebastian?' she heard Hugh say quietly. 'For £50,000, eh? Not really a very high price. But there was a malice factor, eh? That was a mistake, Sebastian. Never mix personal emotions with business. That's my advice to you. Where's the £50,000?'

'I haven't got it. Bullen wouldn't play. He said he hadn't got that much any more—the ransom money had gone back to Hymans. What the hell are you doing? It's true, Dell. I swear it. Blast you, what's the idea?'

She twisted to see. Hugh was ripping with his knife at

Sebastian's clothes, slitting them, tugging them away from his body, to strip him without loosing his wrists. When Sebastian started to shout, Hugh shoved into his mouth a wad of cloth ripped from his shirt, pulling off a sleeve to fasten round his head, securing it.

'Hugh,' Frosso weakly protested. He paid no attention to her.

Suddenly Sebastian's body jerked and writhed in agony. Through the gag he was trying to scream. His head was threshing from side to side. She saw that Hugh's hand was thrust between Sebastian's thighs, grasping his testicles, twisting and punching them. 'For God's sake!' she cried in dismay.

'There are so many simple ways of inflicting pain on the human body,' Hugh told her placidly. 'We often used this one in Africa. It leaves practically no trace.'

Then he stopped. Sebastian's body had collapsed. He had passed out.

Hugh pulled the gag from his mouth and began to slap his face. To Frosso he said sharply, 'Keep watch, as I told you.'

She turned away to scan the darkling countryside. Nobody. She could hear Sebastian moaning as he came to; then retching, vomiting on the floor of the car. When he had finished, Hugh's voice, cold and quiet. 'Is that enough, Sebastian? Are you going to tell me now where the £50,000 is, or will you tell me after the next bout?'

The moans continued. Frosso was seized with a terror that he would not divulge, or perhaps could not, and that filthy thing would happen again.

But then came muttering amid the moaning. She understood that the money would be placed at ten o'clock in a hut at the entrance to a quarry. Bullen had agreed to put it there. Reaching for a map and a flashlight, Hugh was identifying the road and the quarry. 'You're not lying, I hope, Sebastian. If you are, you would be advised to say so now. The next bout would be much less pleasant . . . Very well, we've about an hour to wait. Drive around, Frosso. We'd better not stay too long in one place, it might attract attention.'

He was shoving the cloth back into Sebastian's mouth, leaving him slouched on the floor of the car in his own vomit. The stink was horrible. Frosso let down her side window as she drove slowly off.

'I'll direct you,' said Hugh, who had the map and the flashlight on his lap. 'We'll pull up above the quarry at 10.30. You'll walk down to collect the suitcase, Frosso. Let's hope there won't be any trouble—because if there is, I shan't wait for you. And let's hope,' he added quietly, 'that the suitcase is there. For Sebastian's sake.'

As they reached the hill above the quarry entrance, he told her to stop the car. 'You walk the rest, Frosso. Take the flashlight but don't use it more than you have to. Flash it twice down on to the road just before you enter the quarry. When you come out, flash it on to the road three times, if all's well. Then I'll drive down to pick you up.'

She got on to the road, walking unsteadily, almost sobbing to herself. As she went, her eyes grew accustomed to the night and she did not need to use the flash. Once she was off the road and into the quarry, should she run for it? Anything to get away from those gagged screams, and the sight of Sebastian's body twisting and writhing on the floor of the car, and the stench of the vomit.

But she knew she would not dare. She would do what Hugh told her. She no longer had any independence of him, she knew that. And if she ran in the quarry, there might be no other way out, but only the quarry walls she could not climb—and Hugh Dell coming in after her, moving in that swift, silent manner. Frosso shuddered so profoundly she almost cried out.

At the quarry entrance she used the flashlight for long enough to make out a rough road leading to a small wooden hut. She turned back on to the tarmac of the roadway and flashed the light downwards twice. The sidelights of the car flicked off and on in acknowledgment.

The track in the quarry was so rutted that she stumbled three times, once nearly falling. Outside the hut she stood for a few minutes, paralysed with fright, unable to move. When she opened the door—what? Were they inside, waiting to grab her?

She forced herself to raise her arm, to push gently at the wooden door. It moved, squeaking rustily. She paused, waited. There was no sound.

Desperately she shoved the door open, flashing the light into the hut. On the floor, just clear of the door, lay a suitcase. Otherwise, nothing. And no sound.

With a gasp she grabbed the suitcase, turned, and stumbled back towards the quarry entrance, lugging the case with difficulty. At every moment she expected lights to open up on her, men to come running. But nothing. Only darkness. And silence.

Outside, she flashed the light downwards three times on to the road. She saw the lights of the car move at once. As it drew up beside her, Hugh held open the nearside front door, hoisted the case, and she scrambled in. 'Good girl!'

He drove fast for several miles, then pulled up under trees. 'Time to check.'

Taking the flash, he undid the catches of the case, lifted the lid. The notes were there, fastened into bundles. He smiled, closed the case, started the car forward.

'Straight back to London?' she asked.

He made no reply. She did not repeat the question. She was nearly beyond sensation of anything.

They were following a narrow road across the hump of rolling hills. The Purbecks, she thought. It was a gated road; twice he had to draw up to open a gate, closing it carefully behind him. At last he brought the car to a stop, switched off the engine and got out. She saw him open the rear door and haul Sebastian out on to the grass. His mouth was still stuffed with rag, his hands still bound. But his feet were now naked of shoes and socks, and he was wearing bathing trunks; Hugh must have pulled those on to him while she was in the quarry.

She was watching the scene dimly, not comprehending. There was a noise which she did not at once identify. Then she realized it was the surge of the sea among rocks—and the car was almost at the edge of a cliff.

At that she woke with a cry to what was happening.

Sebastian was wriggling, struggling, trying to break free. But Hugh held him as though in an iron pincer. In his other hand Hugh held a chunk of rock he had picked up from the cliff edge.

'No,' she screamed, fumbling with the car door, trying to rush out to intervene.

But by the time she got round the car, the hand with the rock had smashed twice into Sebastian's skull. His body hung loosely in Hugh's grip. With the third blow, yellow brain material seeped out among his hairs.

Frosso held her fist tightly against her mouth, trying not to scream, trying not to faint.

Hugh severed with his knife the cord that bound the wrists, and pulled the rag from the mouth, carefully prising open the jaw, using the flashlight to make sure that no sizeable scrap of shirt clung to the teeth. Then.

with a quick stoop, lift and thrust, he spun the body well clear of the cliff edge, waiting for the thud as it hit the rocks below. He tossed the piece of rock after it.

She had fallen to the ground, shuddering, sobbing. Hugh illumined her with light from the flash.

'Get up,' he said, quietly but strongly. 'There was no other way. And there is no risk. At high tide the sea covers those rocks. He left his hotel for a bathe and didn't return. In a few days his body will be washed up. Found drowned. His clothes will not be found; they must have been left below high tide mark, and washed out to sea. He'll be identified through the car he hired. There'll be a little police curiosity because he had probably registered in the hotel in a different name—but not much. People who want to disappear, or are having some sort of shady affaire, do that sort of thing all the time. And the garage will tell them about the girl who was enquiring for him and didn't know where he was staying. It will all soon be forgotten.'

She glared up at him. 'It was murder. You killed him.'

'So? I have killed a good many, from time to time.'

She knew, in her despair, that she must get away from him, go to the police; but not for a moment must she let him suspect that.

Yet at once, as though he knew, he told her, 'You're as deeply in it as I. If there were a murder charge, you'd be charged jointly. But there won't be a charge. I tell you, it's all right. Get in the car. We're going back to London.'

She rose listlessly. She could scarcely hold herself erect long enough for him to open the car door, to let her droop on to the seat. He did not at once resume his seat at the wheel. She wearily turned her head and saw that he had pulled the rear carpet from the floor of the car and was wiping as much vomit as he could on to the grass. He threw the carpet back without refastening it. 'Later on I'll burn it, with all his clothes.'

Then he got in and started the car, turning it away from the cliff.

It all spun round and round in her mind as the car travelled, first on to lesser roads, then on to main and, after a time, as day neared, into the early heavy traffic heading for London.

One idea gradually obsessed her. 'Hugh,' she said at last, 'we must get out. We've got the £50,000. That's all. We must get out—get out of the country.'

'Don't panic. You'll feel better when you've had a rest. To run for it now would be the most dangerous possible course.

'Besides, the ransom agreed upon was a quarter of a million. There's another £200,000 to collect.'

After a pause he added, 'There are a few differences, though. One is, there are now only two of us to share it. Another is that we now have to collect it fast—but fast.'

In the first hours of Saturday morning Len Symes happened to emerge from a side street on to the esplanade at Weymouth. He would have been more properly tucked up with Mrs Symes and the two daughters in Sawdon Hall, of course. However . . .

There was a cluster of lights moving about on the beach at the edge of the water, where some fishermen were dragging their boat on to the sands; one was running across the beach to a telephone callbox.

Prudence would have advised Len Symes not to pay any attention, but curiosity impelled him to have a look; after all, he had been doing nothing wrong in Weymouth that night, only looking round as it were, and no tools on him, not so much as a small jemmy or even a strip of cellophane. So he crossed the beach to look.

They were lifting a man's body from the stern of the

boat—naked except for a gaudy pair of swimming trunks that were tangled round the poor chap's knees.

'Found him washed up on some rocks along the coast,' volunteered one of the fishermen. 'Must have swum out too far and not been able to get back. His head's knocked about nasty by the rocks. We get them every year, these bathing fatalities. People are such bloody idiots.'

'Ah,' agreed Len Symes. For he had just recognized the corpse—small-time fence in Chelsea he'd dealt with from time to time, mostly with odds and ends of silver. Hurley, that was his name.

As he turned away to get back to Sawdon Hall before anyone stirred for breakfast, two thoughts occurred to Len Symes.

What occurred to him in the first place was that Sir David was a good old bugger, and had been bloody kind to his missus, and to Kathleen and Grace.

What occurred to him in the second place was it was a funny thing that a small-time Chelsea fence should be found dead, with his head bashed in, rocks or no rocks, fairly close to Sawdon Hall; particularly since there had been a sort of whisper among certain people in London that a Chelsea fence had been mixed up with the theft of that painting of Sir David's said to be worth a couple of million oncers.

CHAPTER XVIII

The Sawdon Arms, in Sawdon Abbas, had put Charles Harrison up very comfortably for the night. He had arrived too late to get in touch with Bullen on the Friday.

The pub produced a decent roast duck and a surprisingly good bottle of claret, reasonably priced, late in the evening though it was. When you found that rare thing, a good English pub, Charles reflected contentedly, there was nothing to complain of. He treated himself to a glass of port with the cheese—rather indifferent port, alas, but an excellent slice of Cheddar—and a brandy with the coffee. Then he went pleasantly ruminant to bed; the mattress was comfortable, the linen worn but spotless, and the landlord had to push aside a cluster of pink roses from the climber on the wall, with an apology, before he could get the bedroom window open. Charles found it delightful. He slept without a break and woke to a huge breakfast of bacon and eggs, toast and local honey, a vast earthenware pot of strong tea. He had scarcely finished when the landlord told him Sir David Bullen wanted to speak to him on the phone.

'Can you come up to the Hall straight away? Rose is driving down to pick you up.'

'Of course. Delighted.'

Bullen was in his office with a thin, furtive little man who had neglected to shave that morning.

'This is Len Symes,' said Bullen. 'He's one of the guests here, with his wife and two little girls. Got turned out of their rooms in London, so we're putting them up for a while. Len saw something odd this morning. He happened to be in Weymouth rather early.' Rose Pearson was frowning, but Bullen smiled at her. 'Len's a very poor sleeper. He saw a drowned man's body brought ashore by fishermen, who had found it among rocks along the coast. Do you know a picture dealer named Sebastian Hurley?'

'Hurley? Why, yes, I vaguely do. He's not much of a dealer—hangs about in the Chelsea fringe. I've run across him a few times at parties and such. Rather an amusing man. Was it Hurley's body? What the devil was he doing bathing at Weymouth?'

'Maybe he was just on holiday,' said Bullen. 'Do you

know where he lived in Chelsea?'

'Can't say I do. Oh, but wait a minute. He had a grotty little antique shop with a silly name, just off the King's Road. I went there once, now I recall it. He had a few English watercolour drawings we sold for him—David Cox and Birkett Foster mostly, if my memory serves. Pleasures—that was it. That's the name of the shop. Typical Chelsea nonsense. I say, what's this all about, then?'

'According to Len, Hurley was a fence as well as a picture dealer.'

'Shouldn't be at all surprised.'

'There's been a rumour that a fence was mixed up in the theft of the Velazquez.'

Harrison stared. 'By all the demons in Hades!'

Bullen was immobile, musing. 'If Hurley was the man . . .'

'Ring the police,' urged Rose.

Slowly Bullen shook his head. 'I think we'll have a look at the antiques shop first. Pleasures, you said, Harrison? Off the King's Road? I'll find it easily enough.'

'Take you to it,' volunteered Charles. 'There are a couple of points I wanted to mention to you. We can talk on the way.'

'Of course. My dear man, I apologize. You've come from London specially to see me.'

Rose Pearson, without a word, got into the car with them. Bullen said nothing either.

He paused at the pub for Charles to pick up his bag and pay his bill. Then he turned to the right off the London road. 'Something I have to check on.'

At the entrance to the quarry he pulled up, walked over to a small hut, peered inside and came back to the car, turning it, making for London now.

'Was that where you handed over the £50,000?' asked Charles.

'You knew?'

'By pure chance. Joe Hymans thought that, as I had introduced you, we knew all about it, and he rang up Syndercombe to thank us. If the money's gone, what happens?'

'I'm supposed to receive, first post on Monday, the names and addresses of a man and a woman who have the painting.'

'Very trusting of you—and of Joe Hymans, too.'

'Calculated risk that, I think, would have come off. But now . . .'

'Now?'

'If Hurley was the man, and he's dead . . .'

Charles sat silent a moment, taking in the implications. Then he murmured, 'Are you saying murder?'

'Not saying anything until we've been to Pleasures.'

Bullen drove with meticulous care, but fast. They were in Chelsea before one o'clock.

There was nobody in the shop except a slatternly woman sitting behind an escritoire, knitting. Mr Hurley? Oh, he wasn't there any longer. Sold the business to Wilf. Going to the inner door, she shouted up the stairs, 'Wilf.'

The thick-set, red-headed man who descended to the shop grew patently cautious when Bullen mentioned Hurley. He had no idea where Hurley was. Yes, he had bought the business, been talking of it for months. Hurley said he was going abroad, but the red-haired man did not know where.

Charles, who had been wandering round the shop peering at the bric-à-brac, suddenly exclaimed, 'That's odd!'

He was holding in his hand a small tarnished silver frame containing a girl's photograph.

'That's the girl who came in here a couple of days ago,' the woman of the shop told him. 'She was looking for Mr Hurley too. Said he'd got some trinket of hers. Had a chap with her, nice-looking fellow. Wilf talked to him.'

'Couldn't help him,' muttered Wilf uneasily.

'Did you know the man? Did they leave any address or anything?'

'Never seen either of them before, or since. And no address. The girl said she'd call back to see if I'd come across her necklace. But I haven't. And she hasn't, neither.'

When they were back in the car, Charles said, 'That's a photograph of my secretary, Frosso Teague.'

The two men stared at each other.

'Oh, but it's impossible,' protested Charles.

'It would make sense of almost everything, wouldn't it?'

Bullen gently closed the car door and drove to Crosby's. The great old place was closed for the weekend, but the watchman let them in. Harrison searched his desk, at last came across an address and a telephone number. He rang it. A girl answered.

'Is that you, Judy? It's Charles Harrison. Is Frosso in?'

'No, Mr Harrison. She hasn't lived here for months ... No, I don't think we have her new address. Somewhere in Chelsea.'

'But you gave me her message that she was unwell.'

'She rang up to say so on Thursday night, and asked me to tell you.'

Harrison, hanging up the phone, idly thumbed his phone-numbers pad. He suddenly realized that the number for Frosso differed from that in the old record in his desk. He pointed it out to Bullen, and they dialled it. The tone rang and rang. After a time he hung up. No reply.

'If the number's been changed, then the new address

must be somewhere in the office,' he declared.

'I'll lay any odds it's not,' Bullen softly replied.

'Can't we get the address of this phone number from the Post Office?'

'Only if you tell the police,' interposed Rose. 'They can. You can't.'

'No,' said Bullen. 'Not yet, anyway. Maybe she'll be in later.'

'She'll be back here in the office on Monday,' said Harrison.

'Maybe.'

Wilf was worried. Only a couple of hours after that lot had left, another fellow came round asking for Sebastian Hurley; and this fellow, quite clearly, was police. Wilf was never wrong about that. So he said as little as he possibly could—just knew nothing.

'Why didn't you tell him about the others round here?' the woman asked when the fellow had gone.

'Tell the police?'

'Was he police? Blimey! What's it all about, Wilf?'

'Damned if I know. But I don't like it.'

'Ah well,' she consoled, 'we don't have to worry. Your nose is clean.'

'Oh sure,' he uneasily agreed. 'Sure it is.'

Detective-Sergeant Madge reported to Foy. Madge was disappointed. When Freddie, after some persuasion by the right officer, and a couple of promises, had murmured they ought to have a word with a little picture dealer in Chelsea named Sebastian Hurley, at a shop called Pleasures, Madge had been elated. He had prophesied that, once they found Boy Shepherd, they'd pick up a continuous trail. And so they had. It had led to Freddie, and thus to Sebastian Hurley and the shop called Pleasures—and there it had ended. Madge was pretty sure that the red-haired man really knew nothing. 'He wasn't comfortable, sir. But then, in that business they don't like people asking questions.'

Foy nodded. 'Routine is usually more effective, Sergeant. Get out an all-stations wanted-for-questioning notice, police circulation only, no publication or intimation, with what little we know of Hurley. No photo, I suppose? We'll scout around for one later. Better duplicate to Interpol—and have a quiet word on the phone with your chum in Dublin. Ireland's the most likely, if he has bolted for it. *If* he has. But why should he?'

Two hours later Madge was back at Foy's desk. 'Reply in from Weymouth, sir. They've got Sebastian Hurley. His body was brought in by fishermen early this morning. He'd been for a swim—still got his bathing trunks on. Found drowned among rocks a few miles east along the coast. Head badly knocked about on the rocks, they say.'

'Identification?'

'He'd hired a self-drive car and produced his driving licence. The car was outside a private hotel where he was registered in the name of Peter Strange. The landlady had reported him missing when he didn't come back last night, and the car linked the two identities. The car-hire garage proprietor says there was a girl enquiring after him yesterday afternoon. Said she was his fiancée, and didn't know which hotel he was staying at. The garage man told her.'

Foy was gently tapping the under edge of his desk with his fingernails, his habit in a moment of excitement. 'Weymouth. Can't be more than ten or fifteen miles from Sawdon Abbas. I believe it's coming together at last, Madge. Get through to Weymouth and tell them one of our medicine men is on his way—and get one moving fast. I want the cause of death, with absolute certainty. If it wasn't drowning, I want to know if death occurred before or after he was in the water. Get started. I'm going to have a word with Bullen. Is he still in Dorset?'

'No, sir. I checked earlier. He came back to London today.'

'Ring him and tell him I'm coming round. I believe the gallant baronet may have a little confession to make.'

While he sat in his office in Battersea, waiting for Foy to arrive, Bullen tried to decide how much he would reveal, and how much admit. Admit only what he had to. Reveal nothing.

Foy was brusquer than he had been before. 'I asked for your co-operation, Sir David.'

'I didn't promise it.'

'I won't start pontificating about a citizen's duty and crime. What I want to impress on you is that people who think they can solve things without police machinery, usually find that they can't. You've had a contact about which you told me nothing.'

Bullen inclined his head. 'On Wednesday I got a typed letter, obviously from the man who sent us his fingerprints.' Bullen took the letter from his desk drawer.

Foy read it without comment. 'Then?'

'I went to see the American dealer, Joe Hymans, and he agreed to risk £50,000.'

'Real money?'

'Yes. He knew it was a gamble, and he took it. I offered him favourable terms on recovery of the Velazquez.'

'Then?'

'I went to Dorset, as instructed. On Friday afternoon there was a phone call from our old friend with the fake scowse accent—the same chap, no doubt, as the fingerprints. He said to leave the money in a wooden hut in a deserted quarry near Sawdon Abbas just after ten o'clock that night.' He stared impassively at the detective. 'This morning, when I checked, it had gone.'

'So now you expect to receive the names and addresses of the man and woman who have the painting? I doubt if you'll get them, Sir David. I have reason to believe that I now know who your contact is—or rather, was. There's still a fingerprint check to come. If I'm right, he was an antiques dealer named Sebastian Hurley, with a shop in Chelsea.'

'You said a fingerprint check.'

'The Weymouth police have got his body. He was brought ashore early this morning by fishermen who found it thrown up by the sea on rocks along the coast. They assumed his head injuries were caused when waves flung him against the rocks. I'm having that checked medically. I believe we shall find that the wounds were caused by blows struck before his body entered the water. In short, I suspect that the man was murdered, probably by his former associates, who must have discovered that he was about to betray them, and who now, presumably, have your £50,000—or rather, Mr Hymans's £50,000. I hope you now realize, sir, what the consequences can be of hiding vital information from the police.'

'I regret nothing, Mr Foy.'

'You don't regret having been the indirect, even if unknowing, cause of a man's death?'

Bullen's steady gaze did not shift. 'What is one man's life, compared with the lives of thousands of men, women and children for years ahead—decades ahead? That's the measure of what the recovery and sale of the Velazquez can accomplish. I will do anything, and accept any responsibility, to get the value of that picture into the Sawdon Trust. If it involves the murder of a criminal, I regret that, of course, but I pay no heed to it.'

'Then I must make my attitude as clear, Sir David. I require you to inform me at once of any further contact you may receive, and to tell me anything that might help to lead us to the people concerned. If you fail to do so, or attempt in any way to impede police action, I shall not hesitate to take any steps whatsoever to prevent your doing so.' He got up to leave. 'My phone will be manned twenty-four hours a day. I expect your full co-operation.'

When he had gone, Rose came from the adjoining room. 'You told him about Mr Harrison's secretary?'

Bullen shook his head.

'Why ever not?' she cried despairingly.

'Because I have one last chance to get that picture back, Rose, and I propose to have a stab at it. If I fail, I'll tell Foy all about it—because by then it will be too late.'

'What last chance?'

'When I got back here, there was another typed message on my desk, in the usual envelope with an 8 on the reverse. It was delivered by a man who came into the hallway earlier and asked one of the kids the way to my office.'

'What was the message?'

He shook his head again. 'I said nothing to Foy about that either, and I'm not telling you what the message is. If it goes wrong, I'll be the only person responsible. And I'm not sure that you wouldn't ring Foy and pass it on to him.' He smiled at her. 'Is that unfair?'

'Perhaps not,' she admitted in a choked voice. Then she turned abruptly away from him and walked uncertainly from the room.

He took the envelope from his desk, re-read the message: 'Be outside Putney Bridge Underground station at 10.00 hours tomorrow, Sunday. Come alone. Bring the £200,000 in used notes in two suitcases. If you follow instructions exactly, you will get the picture back tomorrow morning. It's the last chance. If you fail, or try any deception, it will be destroyed at once and you will never hear from us again.'

CHAPTER XIX

Bullen got there a few minutes before ten o'clock and set down the suitcases on the pavement outside the Underground station. It was hot. The sun was bounding from the roadway in the narrow station approach. He picked up the suitcases and walked round the corner into the main road along which were streaming the cars making for the bridge, and out of London for the Sunday break. There were few pedestrians. A flowerseller was seated by her brilliant basket of roses and gloriosa daisies, near children playing by the parapet. A sculler in a light skiff was zig-zagging over the river surface like a dragonfly; then a purposeful eight, oars rhythmically working, clearing upstream, the cox shouting instructions as each stroke jerked his small body; overhead a few seagulls circling with downward eyes for any edible scum on the water, from which the sunlight glinted and winked.

There was a newspaper seller a few yards down the road. Bullen bought a newspaper, moved back to the station entrance, tried to concentrate on it.

Nobody came near him. It was already 10.20. He tried to pass the time by guessing how the approach would be made. No doubt the man, whoever and wherever he was, meant the delay in order to be sure that Bullen was alone, and not in communication with anybody.

How would the instruction come? He expected it

would be from one of the cars passing in a steady flow along the main road. Probably he would be told to get in and would be driven off. He began to watch the occasional cars turning into the station approach, and so was slightly startled by a boy touching his elbow and offering him a long envelope.

He recovered himself. 'For me?'

' 'Sright. Chap gave me half a quid to give it to you.'

'Where is he?'

The boy shrugged. 'He went round that corner.' He pointed to the turning to the New King's Road. Bullen gave the boy a coin, watched him saunter away, then opened the envelope.

It was an order to view a house for sale, from an agent in Fulham. Five bedrooms, three reception, only one bathroom, large garden, garage. View by appointment only. Asking price for the freehold, £19,750. The address was The Cedars, Middle Gardens, S.W.15.

Bullen walked round to the main road and hailed a passing taxi. 'Know where this is?'

'Over Kingston direction.'

'Okay,' he said, taking his suitcases into the taxi with him.

The house stood well back from a quiet road not far from Richmond Park. Bullen paid off the taxi, picked up the suitcases and pushed open the wide, white gate. It was an ugly red-brick house, built somewhere around the turn of the century. A semi-circular gravel drive led to the front door, and out through another white gate at the far end of a tall, thick patch of laurels, from the midst of which rose two trees, evidently ancient, that had given the house its name. At that end the drive diverted to a garage built against the house.

The silence was almost complete; always the slight hum of distant traffic, but scarcely noticeable in this sheltered place. Bullen walked to the front door in the middle of the house, put down his suitcase and tried it. The door opened. Inside was a large, square entrance hall; wide stairs with an ornate mahogany banister, lit by blue and red light from a stained-glass window on the half-landing. From either side of the hall opened a heavy mahogany door.

Bullen tried the right-hand door; an empty room with a serving hatch beside the littered fireplace, obviously the dining-room. Returning, he crossed the hall and opened the door into the sitting-room. It was a long, empty, white-painted room with a moulded, patterned plaster ceiling.

Over the fireplace hung the *Venus Revealed*.

Bullen walked slowly across to stare up at it, his suitcases still in either hand. He put them down in front of the hearth. From an envelope in his pocket he took the scrap of painted canvas and held it against the tiny, jagged hole in the bottom left-hand corner of the picture. It exactly fitted. It exactly matched. So no expert was needed. This was no copy. This was the Velazquez.

Bullen stared at it again, stepping back a couple of paces. It seemed to him that it was the first time he had really looked at it as a painting, rather than as a money fortune. As he gazed, he began to comprehend the wonder of it. Some girl, three hundred years and more ago, had taken off her clothes and arranged herself, with all the charming, natural grace of a young girl, on a bed with a satin cover; and a painter in Philip's court in Madrid had made this painted picture of her. That the girl herself must have been beautiful was of little importance. At any time there are many thousands of young girls just as lovely, whose fleshly bodies would age and decay, as this girl's had long since. But the essence of her had remained for ever, because the painter happened to be one of the few supreme geniuses of human existence. He had made of the girl's body—the prominent hip, the small exposed breast, the dark hair perfectly piled on a rather sturdy head, the serious look of eyes and grave set of mouth—an expression of the beauty, in all men's eyes, of all young girls. He had painted the desirable and the romantic, the attainable and the unattainable, at once the sensual and the idealized hope of all mankind.

'Perfection, isn't it, Sir David?' came the voice behind him.

Bullen turned slowly. In the open doorway stood a thin man of medium height. His face was hidden behind a red-cheeked-farmer carnival mask of papier-mâché. In his hand he held a small pistol.

Directly David had left Sawdon House that morning, Rose dialled the number that the Superintendent had given him. Foy himself answered.

'I'm Rose Pearson, David Bullen's assistant. He has just gone out to try to get the painting. I don't know where. He had a message last night, but wouldn't show it to me. He said it must be solely his responsibility. But I'm afraid for him, Mr Foy. He has taken two suitcases, which must be supposed to hold the ransom. I don't know what's in them, but it can't be money. He will hate me for having phoned you, but I'm badly frightened for him.'

'Is there any lead you can give me—anything at all?'

'Yes. When we drove up from Dorset yesterday, Mr Harrison was with us. We all went to Sebastian Hurley's antique shop—yes, David knew about Hurley being drowned. One of the thieves at Sawdon Hall happened to see the body being brought ashore, recognized him as a Chelsea fence, and told David, thinking it might have something to do with the painting. So we went to the shop. While we were there, Mr Harrison picked up a photograph of a girl. The woman who now runs the shop said the girl had been in a couple of days earlier, with a man, looking for Hurley. When we got outside, Mr Harrison said it was a photograph of his secretary.'

In the pause she could hear Foy drawing in a long breath.

'Who is she, Miss Pearson? And where is she?'

'Her name's Frosso Teague. That's all I know. We went round to Crosby's, but found she was no longer living at the address recorded for her in the office. But there was another phone number. I'll read it to you.'

Foy repeated it, to make sure, then swiftly handed it to Madge standing beside him, nodding to him to get moving.

'Did you ring it?' he asked Rose.

'David did yesterday, but there was no reply. He hasn't rung it since, because he got the message about a meeting—it must be a meeting, what else? We didn't know the address, and couldn't find it. She's not in the book, or listed ex-directory, I tried that. I wanted David to tell you, because you could get the address straight away from the Post Office.'

'We have a set of reversed directories here, Miss Pearson. My sergeant is looking it up now. Thank you for ringing me. You were absolutely right, of course. Now leave it to us.'

'Can't I join you, wherever you go?'

'Better not. Stay at your office phone. I'll ring you directly I have news.'

As he hung up, he saw Madge returning with the address.

'It's a small block of flats just off Fulham Broadway, sir. Subscriber is the property company that owns the flats. I've asked for a couple of squad cars to be sent there, not to go in, but to follow anybody who comes out before you get there. Your car's waiting down below.'

The sergeant from one of the squad cars reported, when Foy came up, that nobody had left the flats since they had arrived. Foy nodded to Madge to follow him.

It was the flat at the top of the stairs. Foy paused for a moment to catch back his breath, then rang. Silence. He rang again. Silence. But then Madge, listening acutely, whispered, 'There's somebody inside, sir.'

Through the letterbox, which he pushed open with one finger, Foy called, 'Miss Teague. Open the door. This is important. I have a message from Mr Harrison.'

Silence. A long pause. Then a quick, hesitant footstep, and the door ajar, the girl's white face peering out, the eyes black-rimmed.

Madge's shoulder shoved the door. Foy moved in quickly, grasped her wrist and pulled her into the living-room. 'Where is the meeting with Bullen? And where is the painting?'

She was trying hard for calm, but failing, almost paralysed with panic. 'What painting?' she tried. 'What meeting?'

'I haven't time to play games. I know that the painting was taken by you, Sebastian Hurley and two other men. One was the van driver. You probably never saw him. His name is Shepherd—known as Boy Shepherd. He's remanded in custody at Brighton. Sergeant Madge had a long talk with him on Thursday night. Who's the other man?'

'I don't know what you mean.'

Foy chanced his arm. 'We can prove your connection with Hurley—that's how we found our way to you today. Who's the other man? And we know Hurley is dead. His body was recovered from the sea at Weymouth this morning.' He chanced his arm again. 'We know that you were the girl enquiring for Hurley round the car-hire garages at Weymouth. I can't be certain, until I have the medical report that's being worked on now, just how Hurley died. But I shall know. My guess is that I shall then be dealing with a case of murder. Who's the other man?'

Madge pushed a chair under her just in time to stop her falling to the floor. At a nod from Foy, he gave her the usual may-be-used-in-evidence caution. 'Better tell him, Miss.'

She had collapsed forward on to her arms, spread on the small table.

'Who's the man?'

She was weeping now. Through the sobs they caught the name. 'Hugh Dell.'

'Is he meeting Bullen this morning?'

She gave a slight jerk of her head, not lifting her face from its bed on her arms.

Madge took her shoulders and gently raised her, so that she was looking at Foy.

'Has he got the painting with him? He has. Where's the meeting?'

She was regaining control, but she answered the questions. In her terror she could think of no other way. It was as though she could suddenly see Hugh's arm, the lump of rock in his hand, rising and striking, rising and striking; and hear the sea's murmur on the rocks below.

'Where's the meeting?'

'In an empty house up for sale, near Richmond Park. The Cedars, Middle Gardens. I took the painting there early this morning, and Hugh hung it on the wall in an empty room.'

Foy was bristling with suspicion. 'Don't try any games. How could you or Dell know there mightn't be somebody viewing the house, if it's up for sale?'

'It's Hugh's house. He has a property company which owns the house. He wouldn't make any appointments to view today.'

'Same company as owns this block?' put in Madge, quickly.

She nodded.

Madge was getting ready to move, but Foy checked him. 'Just a minute. What is the plan, Miss Teague? What's supposed to happen?'

'If Sir David brings the rest of the ransom, Hugh hands over the picture, and leaves.'

'How?'

'His car is parked in the garage of the house.'

'Stolen car?'

'No, his own. Belongs to the property company. He said it has a right to be there—he has been keeping it garaged there. He said nobody would suspect he stole his own car. I've got the van I carried the picture in this morning. Hugh hired it.'

'Or stole it?'

She shrugged helplessly. 'Maybe. I wouldn't know. I'm to be waiting with it on the other side of Wimbledon Common, half an hour from now.'

'He would arrive in his car, abandon it there, leave in your van—with the picture if he hadn't handed it over to Bullen—and later the company would report that the car had been stolen from the garage. Is that it?'

She nodded.

'And the getaway?'

She was a little calmer, now that she had told them. She accepted automatically a cigarette which Madge offered her, holding a light to it. She gave him a nod of thanks; it was grotesque. 'None—not yet. He said to stay in London. and me in my job, until it had quietened down. Then we'd go in our own time.'

'He was going to ditch you, Miss Teague,' said Foy abruptly, rising. 'Have her taken in the van to the rendezvous, Madge. Couple of uniformed men hidden in the back. Just in case he's already away and makes a run for it.' He turned to the girl. 'What happens if Sir David doesn't produce the money?'

'I wouldn't know,' she protested faintly.

'Put the suitcases flat on the floor and open them, Sir David,' commanded the man in the comic mask.

'There wouldn't be any point,' said Bullen quietly. 'There's no money in them—just old newspapers.'

He saw the hand holding the gun jerk nervously. Then the man's voice came, hard, cold. 'Are you trying to joke?'

'There's no joke. I haven't got £200,000, and I have no chance at all of raising it.'

'You had it before.'

'The police supplied that. The notes were all forgeries. When the ransom attempt failed on the motorway, the police took the notes back. Even if I still had them, I wouldn't have used them. I don't believe that this can be settled by tricks any more.'

'You have already used them.' The man's voice was ugly. 'The £50,000.'

'No, those notes are genuine. I suppose you've got them. I had them from an American art dealer named Hymans, who advanced them on the chance of being able to buy the Velazquez when I recovered it.'

The man had not moved. He was still standing in the doorway. But the gun was slightly moving, restlessly, indecisively, up and down.

'If you haven't brought the money, why have you come? I warn you not to try anything on.'

'I've come to ask you to give me the painting.'

There was a moment's silence, then the man laughed sharply.

'I mean it,' said Bullen. 'Why not? It's now no use to you. There's no chance of the ransom being found. You couldn't sell the picture—certainly not now, when just possessing it automatically convicts you of Hurley's murder.'

'What's that?' The man's voice came in curtly.

'A man staying at Sawdon Hall happened to see the body when it was brought ashore at Weymouth.'

'Brought ashore?'

'Didn't you know? Early yesterday morning. The man knew Hurley as a fence dealing in pictures and silver. Since the £50,000 had been picked up—well, I was guessing. Now you've admitted it.'

'Only to you, Sir David. You won't be telling anybody about it.'

Bullen smiled at him. 'Come now, you're not stupid. You wouldn't commit a second murder if there were a reasonable alternative.'

'Which is?'

'Give me back the painting. You have £50,000, which isn't a bad fee. I will undertake not to reveal for a week that I have the picture, so you will have time to get away. I've not the smallest interest in bringing you to justice, or whatever the cliché may be. All I want is the picture.'

The man laughed contemptuously. 'You said I'm not stupid.'

'I give you my word. What can I do anyway? I can't identify you. I haven't seen your face. All I could say would be a man of middle age, rather short, slim, educated voice. That wouldn't get the police very far.

'I'll make you an even better offer. I'll undertake to describe you as tall, stoutly built, with a Scots accent—anything you like. Be content with the £50,000, and give me back the painting. It's worth nothing to you now —less than nothing, it's a terrible risk to keep it. I need it so much. For me, it's worth a chance for thousands of desperate families. I'm not being sentimental about that. There's nothing sentimental in homelessness, or in children growing up as enemies of society. Give me the painting, and go.'

The man stepped into the room, still with the gun levelled, still keeping a safe distance from Bullen.

'That horse won't run, Bullen. If you won't pay the ransom, somebody else will, some day. The real danger to me is your remaining alive. I regret this, but you asked for it—suitcases stuffed with old newspapers, snivelling nonsense about homeless children . . .'

Bullen, facing the windows, had seen a man moving cautiously along the edge of the drive, in front of the laurels. His face must have given something away, for the masked man suddenly broke off, backed like a lithe animal against the wall and cautiously turned his head sufficiently to glance askew through the window; but the gun never moved from Bullen's direction.

He saw the man outside. To Bullen he snapped, 'Who is it?'

Bullen had just made that out. 'Chief Detective-Superintendent Foy.'

'You bastard!'

'Not that it matters,' said Bullen calmly, 'but in fact I didn't tell the police anything about this morning, and I don't know how they have arrived.'

In his hand Foy held a loud-hailer. Through it he now shouted, 'Dell. Hugh Dell. We know you're in the house.'

'Until this moment,' said Bullen, 'I didn't know your name.'

Foy's voice, loud-hailing: 'This house is surrounded and the police are armed. Come out with your hands on your head, Dell. You can't get away.'

Dell gestured to Bullen to come over to the window, stand where he could be seen. Bullen tried to raise the sash, but it would not budge.

'It's screwed down,' came Dell's voice from behind him. 'But they'll hear you if you shout. The top sash is open.'

'Here, Foy,' shouted Bullen.

But Foy had already seen him, was standing there, irresolute.

Bullen wondered for a moment if he could smash the glass and dive through; but he'd never make it.

Foy through the loud-hailer: 'Are you all right? Is Dell in there with you?'

Dell's quiet, cold instructions: 'Tell them, yes.'

'Yes, he's here. He's behind me. He has a gun. The painting's here too.'

Foy's voice began to address Dell again, urging him to come out. Inside the room, Dell was again instructing Bullen. 'Don't turn round. Keep facing the window. When he stops, tell him that I now have two hostages—the painting, and you.'

The loud-hailer ceased. Bullen shouted, 'He's intending to hold me as hostage, as well as the painting.'

Dell's voice behind him: 'There's a door leading direct from the kitchen into the garage. You will take down the picture, carry it through to the car in the garage, and put it in the back. I shall cover you the whole time. Don't try anything. I'm not squeamish.

'In the garage, put your hands behind you for me to tie. Then get in the front seat. The garage door lifts automatically. When it's open, we shall drive out and through the police cordon. If they attempt to stop me, or follow me, you will be killed. I've made arrangements to change vehicles at a certain rendezvous. Once I'm away, they'll find you eventually, tied up in the car which I shall abandon. If you do as you're told, you will be alive.'

'And the painting?'

'That comes with me. Second line of defence. Now, tell them how we're going to get out of here—but nothing about the second vehicle.'

Bullen turned his head to look back into the room. The man had backed against the wall beside the fireplace, the painting hanging above him.

'Keep facing the window,' snarled Dell. 'Don't turn until I tell you.'

Bullen faced the window again. He felt a great surge of happiness in him.

Raising his voice, he shouted, 'Foy, when I turn away from this window, rush the house.'

He turned deliberately to face Dell, who was now crouching against the wall, gun pointing. The man was panicking. Bullen still could not see his face behind the red-cheeked mask, but there was panic in the man's very crouch.

'You chose the wrong hostage, Dell,' Bullen told him, smiling.

The man's voice was thick. 'Get back. I warn you. Get back.' In his voice there was not only a note of fear, but of uncertainty, as though he was bewildered by the one situation he had not foreseen, the one act to which he had not thought out the counter. 'Get back,' he repeated, his voice rising.

Again Bullen felt the vast, confident joy filling all his mind. He started to move slowly towards the man crouching against the wall.

He felt the bullet hit him in the stomach. Twisting, he managed to grip hold of the window ledge, and to shout, 'Come on in, Foy. Come fast.'

He was mistily aware of men running, feet crunching across the gravel drive. The second shot hit him in the back. He scarcely felt the impact. As he rolled over on the floor, he could just see, before his eyes failed, the serious eyes of the girl in the painting, gazing at him calmly across the centuries, an assurance that, in the end, everything is fitting, all is well.